Sam Connelly looked like a man who would know how to please a woman.

He was shirtless and his dark hair was slightly tousled, as if he'd been in bed.

Daniella's mouth went dry. "Is there something you need?"

"Yeah, there is." He walked toward her with slow, deliberate steps, his gaze never wavering from her. "I need that kiss we talked about earlier."

Daniella knew the difference between right and wrong, and she'd always told herself that it was wrong to get involved in any way with her guests, but at the moment she didn't care. She wanted to be wrong.

She'd expected something simple, something light, but when he reached a hand up to cup the back of her head and pulled her tight against his bare chest, she knew this kiss wasn't going to be anything remotely resembling simple.

CARLA CASSIDY

SCENE OF THE CRIME: BACHELOR MOON

TORONTO NEW YORK LONDON
AMSTERDAM PARIS SYDNEY HAMBURG
STOCKHOLM ATHENS TOKYO MILAN MADRID
PRAGUE WARSAW BUDAPEST AUCKLAND

Dedicated to Annie Hale,

Friend and fellow writer who dreamed of a book called Bachelor Moon.

Annie, I know the angels are now enjoying your stories, basking in the warmth of your soul and delighting in the sound of your laughter. Our loss is Heaven's gain.

ISBN-13: 978-0-373-69525-6

SCENE OF THE CRIME: BACHELOR MOON

Copyright © 2011 by Carla Bracale

Recycling programs for this product may not exist in your area.

ABOUT THE AUTHOR

Carla Cassidy is an award-winning author who has written more than fifty novels for Harlequin Books. In 1995, she won Best Silhouette Romance from *RT Book Reviews* for *Anything for Danny*. In 1998, she also won a Career Achievement Award for Best Innovative Series from *RT Book Reviews*.

Carla believes the only thing better than curling up with a good book to read is sitting down at the computer with a good story to write. She's looking forward to writing many more books and bringing hours of pleasure to readers.

Books by Carla Cassidy

HARLEQUIN INTRIGUE
1077—THE SHERIFF'S SECRETARY
1114—PROFILE DURANGO
1134—INTERROGATING THE BRIDE*
1140—HEIRESS RECON*
1146—PREGNESIA*
1175—SCENE OF THE CRIME: BRIDGEWATER, TEXAS
1199—ENIGMA
1221—WANTED: BODYGUARD
1258—SCENE OF THE CRIME: BACHELOR MOON

*The Recovery Men

CAST OF CHARACTERS

Sam Connelly—The burned-out FBI agent wasn't looking for love and he definitely wasn't looking for murder.

Daniella Butler—She runs a bed-and-breakfast and has become a killer's obsession.

Mary Marie Butler—Daniella's precocious five-year-old daughter is convinced she can turn Sam into the third princess in her little operation.

Johnny Butler—Daniella's ex-husband. He'd disappeared years ago. Was he back now with a score to settle?

Matt Radar—He was reputed to have killed his wife. Was it possible he had another victim in his sights?

Frank Mathis—Daniella depended on the handyman to keep things running smoothly. Did he harbor dark secrets that nobody knew?

Jeff Tyson—He and Daniella's ex had been best friends, but now he seems to want more than just friendship from Daniella.

Chapter One

If he'd agreed to see the FBI psychiatrist like his boss had wanted, this was probably what the doctor would have ordered.

That was the first thought that jumped into Sam Connelly's head when he pulled up in front of the Bachelor Moon Bed and Breakfast.

Located ten miles from the small town of Bachelor Moon, Louisiana, the huge two-story house was surrounded by large cypress and maple trees and sported a large sweeping veranda. The website had indicated that the house had three guest quarters inside and an additional three in a renovated carriage house.

As Sam parked his car and got out he was greeted with the blessed sound of nothing but nature at work. A bird sang from one of the trees as a light breeze rustled through the branches. Somewhere from the distance he heard a faint splash from the huge pond on the side of the house that the website claimed was stocked with catfish and bass.

Yes, this was just what the doctor would have ordered: two weeks of peace and quiet, fourteen days of thinking about nothing more difficult than what bait to use. He supposed he needed a break from the darkness that had been his life for so long. In truth there were times when he felt as if he'd swallowed a whole night full of darkness.

He stretched his arms overhead. The drive from Kansas City to Bachelor Moon, Louisiana, should have taken only about nine hours, but road construction had added an additional two hours to the trip.

The bed in the motel room where he'd stayed the night before had been abysmal, and he'd gotten little sleep. If he thought about it he could get downright cranky.

This vacation had been forced on him, and Sam didn't like the idea of time off or anyone telling him what he needed to do. As an FBI profiler he knew that the serial killers he hunted certainly didn't take vacations.

With a sigh he accepted the here and now and grabbed his duffel bag from the backseat. Although it was just after ten in the morning, already the sun beat hard on his shoulders and the humidity pressed tight against his chest.

At that moment the front door of the house swung open and a woman appeared on the veranda. She wore a long, dark blue, gauzy skirt that the breeze swirled around her slender legs, and a light blue sleeveless blouse that exposed lightly tanned arms and emphasized the press of full breasts.

Long blond hair framed a heart-shaped face, and the

smile of welcome that curved her lips caused a flicker of something alien deep inside Sam.

"Hello," she said as he approached. "You must be Mr. Connelly."

"Sam. You can call me Sam," he replied. As he drew closer he realized that she wasn't just pretty, but she had the kind of classic beauty that required little makeup or artifice. Her eyes were the blue of a summer sky, and her features were elegant without being cold.

"I'm Daniella Butler, owner and operator of this place." She opened the front door wide to allow him inside.

He swept past her and into a large foyer, aware of the scent of ripened peaches that either came from her or rode in the air inside the house.

"I'll just show you around and then take you up to your room," she said.

He nodded, vaguely surprised by his instant attraction to her. God, he couldn't remember the last time he'd felt anything for anyone. He'd turned off his emotions a long time ago.

"This is the common room," she explained as she led him into a large family-room-type area. There was a television, a bookshelf with books, puzzles and games, a table and a sofa and several easy chairs. "It's just a place to hang out if you're feeling sociable."

The one thing he didn't intend to feel while he was here was sociable, he thought, as she led him into the next room, a large dining area.

"This is where meals are served," she continued.

"Breakfast is from seven to nine, lunch is eleven to one and dinner is five to seven." Her voice had the soft drawl of somebody born and bred in the region. "On Sundays the only meal I serve is breakfast, but there's plenty of dining places in town. I also try to keep little nibbles in the common room if you get the munchies between meals."

She offered him another warm smile, and he forced his lips to stretch in what he hoped was a smile of his own. It had been so long since he'd smiled at anyone the gesture felt forced and strange.

"Now, if you'll follow me, I'll show you to your room," she said.

As he followed her up the wide staircase he tried not to notice the sway of her shapely hips before him. Normally, his head was filled with crime scene reports and grisly details of murders. He couldn't remember the last time that his head had been empty enough to enjoy the view of a woman's swinging hips, the weight of a fishing pole in his hand, the simple things that everyone told him made life worth living.

"Is it always this quiet?" he asked once they had reached the second-floor landing.

She turned to face him. "On the weekdays it's fairly quiet. I have one man who has been staying here for the past two months, but other than that the place only fills up on the weekends and then things get a little livelier. So, that gives you the next three days to enjoy the peace and quiet, if that's what you're after."

She gestured him into a room on her right. The large,

airy bedroom was painted soft green with white borders. The four-poster bed looked as if it had one of those pillowy mattresses that instantly made Sam's muscles moan in sweet anticipation.

He set his duffel bag on the floor and moved to the window to look outside. From this vantage point he could see a wooden walkway, which led to a dock, and a pond almost big enough to be considered a lake, which sparkled in the morning sunshine.

"The bathroom is here," she said, drawing his attention away from the window. "And here's the key to the room. Unfortunately the days of unlocked rooms in a bed-and-breakfast are over."

He took the key she held out to him and noticed that she wore no wedding ring. Not that it mattered. Not that he cared in the least. There was only one thing he wanted to know from her. "What's the best bait to use?"

"Worms or crawdads," she replied. "And I don't clean what you catch, but I'll be glad to cook it up for you if you want. There's a shed in the backyard that has bait and a place to clean fish, and you're welcome to help yourself. Just let me know if you need anything else and once again, welcome to Bachelor Moon."

He was grateful when she left him alone. Being sociable and pleasant had never been one of Sam's strong suits. What Sam did best was crawl into the mind of killers.

"Not here, not now," he muttered to himself as he opened his duffel bag and began to unpack.

It took him only minutes to store the jeans and T-shirts he'd brought with him in the dresser drawers. Then he left the room and went back downstairs, intent on spending the rest of the day with a fishing pole in his hand.

He didn't see Daniella as he went back down the stairs although he heard the murmur of voices coming from another room. He walked back out the front door and to his car, where he grabbed a new fishing pole and tackle box from the trunk.

He'd been fishing only a couple of times in his life, the last time over twenty-five years ago, when he'd been about ten. At that time he'd gone fishing with his best friend and his best friend's father. It had been one of the few good memories he had of his childhood.

He found the shed where Daniella had indicated bait was kept. Inside the cool, dark interior an old refrigerator hummed; it stored foam containers of fat worms. Crickets chirped from a cage, and a dank tank held crawdads. There was also a wooden table with a water spigot and a trough for cleaning the daily catch.

Sam grabbed a container of worms and tried to keep his mind empty as he walked down the wooden walkway that led to the dock at the edge of the pond. The dock held several lawn chairs. He grabbed one and positioned it facing outward, then eased down and drew in a lungful of the warm, humid air.

He didn't want to be here. He wanted to be in the field, hunting bad guys and getting them off the streets.

He grabbed a worm and looped it onto his hook, then cast out into the sparkling pond.

His coworkers called him the Prince of Darkness because of his ability to creep into the mind and soul of evil. "You're immersing yourself too deeply in your work," Assistant Director Ken Walt had told him three days ago. "You need some time off, Sam. You need some distance, a reminder that there's still good out in the world. You might not know it but you're on the verge of permanent burnout from life."

Sam had argued that he was fine, but ultimately he was given a choice: go talk to the company psychiatrist or take a vacation. So here he was, sitting on a dock wishing he were back on the job.

"If you cast closer to the shore, you'll have better luck."

Sam jumped at the voice coming from just behind him and turned to see a little girl in overall shorts and a red T-shirt, her long blond hair escaping from pigtails. It was a no-brainer who the kid belonged to; she looked just like her pretty mama.

"Thanks, kid, but I'm doing fine." He turned back to stare out at the water, not wanting to encourage any further conversation.

"But if you want to catch fish you should do like I tell you," she replied, and sidled up next to him. "Frank says the best fish in the world like to hide in those big cattails by the shore."

The last thing Sam wanted was a fishing lesson given

to him by a five- or six-year-old. "I'm doing just fine, thanks."

"Suit yourself," she replied. "But if you catch a big old catfish then Mommy can fry it up for supper, and there's nothing better than Mommy's fried catfish."

"I'm not going to catch much of anything if you keep talking. You'll scare all the fish away."

She giggled, a pleasant, childish sound. "Silly boy. Fish don't have ears and you sound a little bit crabby."

"I *am* just a little bit crabby," he replied, hoping that would end the conversation and she'd go find somebody else to talk to.

"Well, you can just get happy in the same pants you got crabby in," she exclaimed.

An unexpected burst of laughter escaped him, the sound rusty from lack of use. She grinned, pleased that she'd made him laugh.

"I'm Macy Marie Butler," she continued. "And I'm a little princess. My mommy is a big princess, and you don't have to be scared of monsters when we're around."

"And why is that?" Sam asked, despite his desire to be left alone.

"Monsters don't have any power when there are princesses around."

"Macy Marie!" Daniella's voice drifted to them from the back porch.

"Uh-oh. I'm in big trouble now." The little girl released a deep sigh. "Here she comes and she's gonna yell at me. I might even get a time-out."

Sam turned to see Daniella coming down the walk, the skirt swirling with each determined stride she took. When she reached them she gave her daughter a stern look. "Macy, go on and get to your room. You know you aren't supposed to bother the guests."

"She wasn't bothering me," Sam surprised himself by saying. "In fact, I was probably bothering her by asking so many questions about the fishing."

Daniella eyed him dubiously, but Macy gave him a beatific grin. "And I was explaining to him about monsters and that you and I are princesses," Macy added.

Daniella's cheeks flushed with color, and once again Sam was struck with a tiny flicker of heat in the pit of his stomach. God, the woman had a smile that could sizzle an egg in a cold skillet.

"Yes, well, this little princess needs to get inside and clean her room," she said, and gave Macy a pat on her bottom.

As Macy ran toward the house Daniella looked at Sam once again. "The princess thing—it started as a story to help with her nightmares of monsters." She looked decidedly uncomfortable.

"So I guess that means you don't want me to call you Your Highness," Sam said. He began to wind in his fishing line.

"Definitely not," she replied with a small laugh.

"Still, it's nice to know you have the monster thing under control."

"Thankfully in Bachelor Moon we don't have to worry much about monsters. Can I bring you a glass of iced tea or something?" she asked, obviously eager to change the subject.

He shook his head. "No, I'm fine." He cast his line out closer to the shore where Macy had indicated he should be fishing.

"Again, I apologize for my daughter. She can be a bit of a handful."

"Nothing to apologize for," Sam assured her. "Besides, I'm sure she's the apple of her daddy's eyes."

Her eyes darkened. "I divorced my husband a year ago. Enjoy the rest of the morning and we'll see you inside for lunch." She didn't wait for a reply but instead turned on her heel and hurried back toward the house.

Sam watched her until she disappeared into the house, then turned back and stared out at the pond. The whole bed-and-breakfast thing was a pretty big operation for a single mother.

Of course, just because she wasn't married didn't mean she was all alone. A woman as gorgeous as Daniella Butler probably had any number of men willing to step up and help her in whatever way she needed.

Sam wouldn't mind helping her if she needed a body to warm her bed. He definitely found her physically attractive, and it had been way too long since Sam had been with any woman.

Monsters. Sam didn't worry much about the monsters he encountered in his work. What he worried about was the monster he feared slept deep in his soul, a monster that might awaken at any moment.

DANIELLA STOOD AT THE back door and stared at the back of her newest guest. Hot. The man was definitely hot, with his slightly shaggy black hair and intense blue eyes.

When he'd first gotten out of his car and had stretched, she'd watched from the door and admired the width of his broad shoulders, emphasized by his lean torso and long legs.

Even though she'd officially sworn off men years ago, that didn't mean she couldn't lust after a particularly handsome specimen when he was right under her roof.

She told herself the slight flush of heat she felt was from the corn bread cooking in the oven and not from speaking with Mr. Hunky Sam Connelly.

Thinking about her corn bread, she opened the oven door to check on it. Dinner this evening would be a traditional gumbo with corn bread. Lunch would be chicken salad croissants with potato salad and coleslaw. It would only be Sam for lunch. Her long-term guest, Matt Rader, was rarely here for the noon meal.

When Daniella had opened the bed-and-breakfast she'd decided to offer three meals to her guests. She loved to cook and adding the additional meals meant she could also make a little money on the food.

And money was always an issue, so she was pleased that for the next month she was pretty well booked solid for the weekends.

Johnny would be so proud. The words jumped unbidden into her mind. As always, thoughts of her ex-husband brought with them myriad emotions that ranged from anger, to grief, to an uneasy lack of closure that might always haunt her.

The knock on the back door shoved thoughts of Johnny right out of her head. Frank Mathis peered in through the screen, and she motioned him inside.

"That flower bed on the north side of the house is looking pretty dismal," he said. "I thought I'd head into town and pick up a couple of new plants to add in. Is there anything you need from the stores?"

She smiled at Frank, who had been her right-hand man since she'd bought the place a little over five years ago. He could make a flower bloom as easily as he could fix the temperamental air conditioner. "No, I think I'm good until Sunday when Macy and I will do some grocery shopping, but let me get you some money for the new plants."

Frank raised a hand to dismiss the offer. "I'll take care of it. I still have some of the money left that you gave me to replace those shrubs in the front."

"Thanks, Frank. And you might want to plan to eat dinner here tonight. I'm making gumbo."

He patted the slight paunch at his middle. "You know I love your gumbo. I'll definitely be here."

As Frank left through the back door, Daniella pulled her corn bread from the oven and thought about the man who had been such a support when Johnny had disappeared and she'd been left alone to run this place.

Frank had worked with Johnny at a factory that manufactured furnace boilers. Two months before Daniella and Johnny had opened the doors to her bed-and-break-fast the factory had closed down, leaving Frank and many other men in the small town unemployed.

Frank had come to them and confessed that he was broke and needed to move out of the apartment he'd been renting. He knew they had a caretaker's cottage across the pond, and he'd sworn that for free rent and board he would take care of whatever needed to be done around the place. Two months later Johnny was gone, but Frank had proven himself invaluable around the place. And it was an added bonus that he adored Macy.

She found herself once again standing at the back door and staring out at her latest guest. Even though he was still seated in the chair she sensed a tenseness about him, a simmering energy that she'd noticed the moment she'd introduced herself to him.

She closed her eyes and for a moment could imagine his strong arms wrapped around her, the spicy scent of his cologne on her skin, in her bedsheets. It had been so long since she'd been held in the warmth of an embrace, felt the breathless excitement of making love.

Sam Connelly looked like a man who would know how to please a woman. There had been a dark heat in his eyes as his gaze had slid the length of her, a sultry heat that had made her feel all tingly inside.

She snapped her eyes open and moved away from the window. What on earth was she thinking? It was ridiculous to fantasize about a guest, even one who looked like Sam.

One of her cardinal rules was to never get involved

with her guests. Sam Connelly was just like all the other people she allowed into her life—fleeting and definitely temporary.

The ring of the phone pulled her from her crazy thoughts. As she went to the desk in the kitchen to answer, she noticed that the caller ID indicated the call was anonymous.

It wasn't unusual for her to get anonymous calls. Some people called to find out the rates and information about the bed-and-breakfast and didn't want her to have their number. They were probably afraid she'd make follow-up calls to them and try to talk them into a vacation they didn't want.

"Bachelor Moon Bed and Breakfast," she said into the receiver. There was a long moment of silence, although she could tell the line wasn't dead. "Hello?"

"For you."

The voice sounded strange, as if it had been somehow altered. "Excuse me?" Daniella replied. There was a soft click and she knew the caller was no longer on the line.

She hung up the phone with a frown. *For you.* What in the heck did that mean? Maybe she hadn't heard right.

She tried to dismiss the call from her mind, knowing it was time to get lunch prepared. Still, as she got busy setting the dining room table for Sam's lunch, she couldn't stop the dark sense of foreboding that slithered through her.

Chapter Two

Sam fished through the lunch hour. He had a couple of bites but never landed a single fish. It didn't matter. As the day wore on and the peaceful silence of his surroundings seeped through him he began to relax in a way he hadn't done in years.

Not once did the details of a case enter his mind. Not once did he think about any of the killers he'd hunted and caught in his career. He just breathed in the air, napped for a few minutes and relaxed.

By four o'clock the late July sun was at its hottest, and he decided to call it a day and head inside to his room. He stored his fishing pole and tackle box in the trunk of his car and went into the house.

He saw nobody as he climbed the stairs to his room, but the air was redolent with the scent of cooking, and he immediately thought of the woman who would be his landlord for the next two weeks.

He certainly wouldn't be averse to a little vacation romance as long as she was willing and able and understood the meaning of *temporary*. It was the only kind of relationship he had—hot and very, very temporary.

Minutes later he stood beneath a shower, grateful that the water pressure was good and the water steamy hot. He hoped the food was as good as it smelled. He regretted missing lunch because now he was starving.

Once he was out of the shower he dressed in a clean pair of jeans and a short-sleeved, light blue, button-up shirt, then stood at the window in his room and stared outside.

Today had been surprisingly pleasant, and he reluctantly admitted that maybe he had needed a vacation after all. He couldn't remember when he'd taken any time off work over the last five or six years.

He was about to walk out of his room and head down to the dining area when his cell phone rang. A glance at the caller ID let him know it was Special Agent Jenna Taylor.

"Is this my favorite prince of darkness?" she asked when he answered.

"Hey, Jenna, what's going on?" he asked, as he sat on the edge of the bed.

"I just wanted to check in with you and make sure you arrived at your vacation paradise okay."

Six profilers worked out of the Kansas City FBI offices. Misunderstood by most civilians, branded as renegades within their department, they were a tight group with a bond that went beyond their jobs.

All of them were single, but when Jenna had traveled to Bridgewater, Texas, to investigate the murder of her best friend, she'd fallen for the local sheriff and was now in the process of transferring from the office in Kansas City to one in Texas.

"I'm here and have spent the day sitting in a chair with a fishing pole in my hand," he replied.

"Good for you. You need this, Sam. You were on your way to falling so far into the darkness that nobody could have pulled you out."

"Whatever," he replied, already faintly irritated by the conversation.

"Seriously, Sam. You need balance in your life. You've got to get some good in with the bad, and it wouldn't hurt if you'd find a nice woman to spend time with."

"You know how I feel about that, so don't even get me started," he replied. "I like being alone and I intend to stay that way."

"I know, but as someone who has just found the love of my life I wish all my friends could feel the same kind of happiness that I have."

Sam sighed. Former smokers and the newly in love, they could both be irritating with their need to reform the entire world. The two talked for another few minutes and then ended the call.

As he walked downstairs to find the evening meal, he shoved thoughts of Jenna from his mind. He was going to miss working with her, but he was glad that she'd apparently found her soul mate.

Despite the fact that he'd found her attractive and had enjoyed working with her, there had never been any sparks between them. They had simply been coworkers who had become close friends.

All thoughts of Jenna left his mind as he entered the dining room to find two men already there. One of them stood near a sideboard pouring himself a cup of coffee from the urn on top, and the other was already seated at the table.

The man at the table stood as Sam entered the room. "You must be the new guest. I'm Matt Rader, a fellow guest of this great place." He held out his hand to Sam.

"Sam Connelly," Sam replied, as he shook Matt's hand.

"I'm Frank, the handyman and gardener and general jack-of-all-trades," the other man replied. "I saw you out on the dock earlier. Did you have any luck?"

"A few nibbles, nothing more." Sam sat in one of the empty seats at the large table, assuming there was no seating assignment.

Frank took a seat opposite Sam. He was an older man—Sam guessed he was in his late forties—and he had the weathered features of a man who spent a lot of time outside. "You here on business or pleasure?"

"Strictly pleasure," Sam replied. "I'm on a two-week vacation and looking forward to doing nothing more strenuous than fishing."

For the next few minutes the men talked about the fishing in the area and the hot weather. Sam was grateful that neither man asked him what he did for a living.

It had been his experience that people did one of two

things when they learned he was an FBI agent. They either got paranoid and distant or they glommed onto him with endless, mostly stupid questions.

The superficial conversation was just beginning to wind down when another man arrived. He was a handsome blond with brown eyes, and he introduced himself as Jeff Tyson, a family friend of Daniella's.

It was obvious the minute Daniella bustled into the room carrying a large bowl of jambalaya that Jeff wouldn't mind being more than a family friend to Daniella. He immediately leaped forward to take the bowl from her, and from the expression on his face Sam knew the man was in love with her.

As Sam saw her a slight sizzle again went through him. Her gaze met his and a hint of color crept into her cheeks. Did she feel it, too? The crazy tug of physical attraction? Maybe her cheeks were just flushed from cooking, he thought as she disappeared back into the kitchen. Or maybe there was something more going on between her and Jeff than just friendship.

She returned a moment later with a pan of corn bread and a bowl of salad. "I have fresh peach cobbler for dessert," she said. "Enjoy your meal."

The food was terrific and the conversation flowed easily between the three men. Sam ate and only half-listened as his thoughts returned to the woman who had served them.

Apparently Daniella and her daughter didn't share their meals with the guests. As the owner of a bed-

and-breakfast, Daniella had certainly set herself up for a demanding life, and she was a single parent to boot.

He had a feeling beneath the sexy package there had to be some major inner strength. It was Sam's experience that divorcees reacted to their life experiences in two ways: either they were eager to get married again and try for the happily-ever-after they'd been deprived of in their first marriage, or they turned their back on the very idea of a second marriage.

There was a small part of him that hoped she fell into the second category, that she was ripe for a very brief, very physical relationship with no emotional attachment, and that she and Jeff truly were just old friends with nothing else going on between them.

He frowned irritably, wondering why he suddenly had sex on the mind. He knew part of the problem was that he'd been so long without it. It had been eight months since he'd been with a woman, part of a fling with a career-minded woman he saw on an irregular basis.

Ramona Welch lived in Topeka and occasionally traveled to Kansas City for business. Whenever she was in town she'd call Sam and they hooked up for the night. There were no expectations between them and definitely no love.

He was grateful when the meal had ended and he escaped to his room after telling the others good-night. He was tired after the long drive that morning and the previous night of little sleep.

After pulling down the pretty green bedspread he stretched out on the bed and considered turning on the television, but decided instead to just enjoy the silence.

There had been little silence in his life or in his head in the last seven years since he'd become a profiler at the age of twenty-eight. His head had been filled with the voices of victims and the whispers of killers, and now, with no pending case to think about, he relished the blessed silence. As much as he hated to admit it, his boss had been right. He'd needed some time away from his job.

He must have drifted off to sleep, for a soft knock on his door awakened him. Instantly he sat up and swung his legs over the edge of the bed. "Yes?" he called.

The door creaked open and Macy peered in. "Can I ask you something?"

He got up from the bed and met her at the door. "What's that?"

"You got any kids?"

"No. Why?"

She shrugged. "Just wondering, that's all. My daddy got lost when I was a baby."

"He got lost?" What did that mean?

Macy nodded. "Mommy told me she looked and looked for him, but we never could find him."

It sounded like a case of abandonment. Despite the hard shell he always kept around his heart he felt a tiny crack as he gazed into Macy's childish eyes.

"Since we can't find him I'm kind of looking for a new daddy."

Before Sam could reply a scream ripped through the

air. Sam instantly recognized it as Daniella and without thought he scooped Macy up in his arms and took the stairs two at a time.

He found her in the kitchen. She stood at the back door, her face white as horror radiated from her eyes. The sight of Macy seemed to center her as she stepped away from the door and some of the color flooded back into her cheeks.

"Macy, go to your room and get ready for bed. I'll be in to kiss you good-night in just a few minutes." Despite the fact that she appeared more calm, Sam heard the tremble in her voice.

Sam placed Macy on the floor. "Why did you scream?" she asked her mother.

"It's nothing, honey. Go on and get your pajamas on and don't forget to brush your teeth."

The minute the child disappeared through a doorway at the back of the kitchen, the horror once again filled Daniella's blue eyes. "Out there…oh, God, she's dead."

Sam stepped out the back door, where the bright porch light illuminated half the yard. The first thing he saw was a trash bag lying on the ground about ten yards from a large Dumpster. The second was the body propped against the base of a large tree.

He sucked in his breath as he went closer to investigate. It was obvious she was dead. A wood-handled knife protruded from the center of her chest, and her brown eyes were frozen open as if in startled response.

She'd been pretty in life. Her dark hair shone with a

rich luster, and her features were dainty and attractive. She was clad in a navy sundress and matching sandals, and Sam instantly ruled out robbery, for her diamond rings were still on her fingers.

He took a step closer, although not so close that he might contaminate the scene. The dried blood around the wound indicated to him that she'd been dead for a while. No blood in the general area led him to believe this was just the dump site, not the scene of the murder.

The grass around where she sat looked undisturbed, with nothing out of place to capture his attention. No gum wrapper, no cigarette butt, nothing that could supply a clue as to who was responsible.

Not your scene, a little voice whispered in his head. *This isn't your problem. You're on vacation.* He backed away. The last thing he wanted to do was get involved. He was simply a guest here; there was absolutely no reason for him to get involved in this crime.

As he turned and saw Daniella silhouetted in the doorway, he hoped to hell he could hang on to his desire to remain uninvolved, but he had a sinking feeling in the pit of his stomach.

DANIELLA WATCHED AS SAM headed back toward the house. She felt sick as wave after wave of horror washed over her. As Sam entered the kitchen she fought the irrational impulse to run into his arms, to feel the warmth of his body against hers.

"I called the sheriff. He should be here soon." She was appalled to hear the quiver in her voice.

Sam took her by the arm and led her to a chair, where she sat and fought back tears. "I was going to take out the trash," she said. "I'd only taken a couple of steps outside when I saw her." She fought against a shudder than threatened to consume her body.

"Do you know her?"

She nodded. "Her name is Samantha Walker. She's the divorced daughter of the mayor of Bachelor Moon." She wrapped her arms around herself in an attempt to ward off the cold horror that still swept through her. "I can't imagine who did this or what she was doing on my property."

"Where is everyone else?" He sat in the chair next to hers and the scent of his clean, crisp cologne swept over her. It was oddly comforting.

"Frank and Jeff went home right after dinner, and Matt went out. Surely you don't think any of them had anything to do with this?"

"I was just curious who was in the house. It looks like she was moved here after she was killed, and she's been dead for quite a while."

Daniella felt the burn of tears as a vision of Samantha filled her head. "I've never seen somebody like that… dead…murdered." She fought against a shudder as Macy came into the kitchen clad in her pajamas.

She jumped up from her chair and pasted a smile on her face. "All ready for a tuck-in?"

"Yeah, but I want Mr. Sam to tuck me in, too." She

grabbed Sam's hand and tugged at him. "Come on, I'll show you my princess crown."

Sam looked shocked, but rose to his feet, obviously understanding that Daniella wanted Macy in bed as soon as possible and not out here when the sheriff arrived or where she might get a peek at Samantha's body.

Macy pulled Sam through the doorway that led to their private quarters. There was a sitting room, a bathroom and two small bedrooms. She followed them into Macy's bedroom where the little girl crawled into the twin bed, pulled up the pink flowered sheet and patted the mattress beside her. "Here, have a seat, Mr. Sam."

Sam looked at Daniella, obviously uncomfortable with the whole scene. Still, he eased down on the mattress as Daniella nodded. Macy opened the drawer in her nightstand and withdrew her glittery princess crown.

It was a surreal moment, her daughter proudly showing off her crown while a dead woman lay in the yard. Samantha Walker wasn't the nicest woman in the world, but Daniella couldn't imagine somebody wanting to murder her. And why had her body been left here?

"You want to see me wear my crown and do my princess walk?" Macy asked Sam.

"It's bedtime now," Daniella said firmly. "There will be another time to show off your princess walk."

"It's a pretty crown," Sam said, as he stood.

"Thank you. It keeps away monsters," Macy replied.

Daniella took the crown from her daughter and placed it back in the drawer. "Good night," she said, then kissed Macy's sweet cheek. "Sleep tight."

"Good night, princess," Sam said. A moment later he and Daniella left the bedroom and went back into the kitchen. "Will she get out of bed again?" he asked.

"I doubt it." Daniella sat in one of the chairs at the small oak table and wondered what was taking the sheriff so long. "Macy has always been one of those unusual kids who loves to sleep. Bedtime has never been a problem with her."

As he sat in the chair next to her, she was overwhelmed by myriad emotions. "I'm so sorry that this has happened," she said. "This isn't business as usual for the bed-and-breakfast."

He smiled, and once again she was struck by his handsomeness. "I didn't think you arranged this scene strictly for your guests' entertainment," he said.

"I just can't believe this is happening." She felt sick, as if she'd never be able to dispel the vision of Samantha from her brain.

At that moment a knock came from the front door, and Daniella steeled herself not only for the investigation to come but also to deal with Sheriff Jim Thompson, who she thought was a cranky incompetent.

She was grateful for Sam's presence just behind her as she opened the door to let Jim inside. "I hope this isn't some sort of wild goose chase," he said as he stepped into the foyer.

"I doubt if the dead woman beneath the tree on the side of the house considers this a wild goose chase," Sam replied.

Jim drew himself up to his banty-rooster height and narrowed his eyes. "And you are?"

"Sam Connelly. I'm a guest here."

"Jim, she's been stabbed," Daniella said. "It's Samantha Walker."

Jim's grizzly gray eyebrows pulled together in a frown. "There's going to be hell to pay with the mayor. Point me in the right direction and let's get this investigation underway."

They were all silent as they walked through the kitchen and Daniella pointed out the door. Sam followed Jim outside while she remained in the kitchen, the horror of the situation back in the center of her brain.

She sat at the table and closed her eyes, but instead of thinking about poor Samantha Walker she found her head filled with thoughts of Sam Connelly. Maybe because it was easier to think about how hot he was instead of how dead Samantha was.

And he *was* hot. It wasn't just the fact that his tight jeans showcased slim hips, long legs and a tight butt, and his shoulders appeared wide enough to shoulder any trouble that might come his way. His electric blue eyes held a keen intelligence and a whisper of darkness that was daunting but also intriguing.

She frowned and rubbed the center of her forehead where a headache attempted to blossom. Something about Sam Connelly struck her on a strictly feminine level, made her remember that she was not only a healthy woman with desires, but also a very lonely woman.

The loneliness had grown more intense over the last

year, when she'd finally given up ever hearing from her husband, Johnny, again. Sure, she had Macy and Frank and Jeff to fill some of the empty spaces in her life, but they couldn't take the place of warm arms wrapping around her in the middle of the night, of that special smile that passed between lovers, of those moments of knowing you were in somebody's heart, in their very soul, as they were in yours.

She mentally kicked herself. She didn't know anything about Sam Connelly other than that he was from Kansas City and he'd paid for his accommodations here in advance with a major credit card. She didn't know what he did for a living, what kind of man he was at heart, or if he had a significant other somewhere.

She got up from the table, moved to the back door and peered out. Sam and Jim stood to one side. Several other deputies had arrived, along with Dr. Earl Stanton, who in addition to his private practice, also worked as the coroner in the area.

Poor Samantha. Who could have done something so terrible to her? Certainly Samantha hadn't been particularly well-liked by a lot of the people in town, but she hadn't deserved this.

Murdered.

She'd been murdered. The horror once again struck Daniella like a fist in the pit of her stomach. It was like a nightmare, and she desperately wanted to wake up.

As she saw Sam and Jim start in the direction of the house, she backed away from the door. Both men looked grim as they came back into the kitchen.

"Earl thinks she was killed sometime early this afternoon at another location then left here," Jim said. "Did she come out here to talk to you?"

"No, Samantha and I had no business with each other, and she rarely acknowledged me when we'd bump into each other in town. I can't imagine why she's here," Daniella replied.

For the next thirty minutes the sheriff asked her questions about her activities that day, about how she had discovered the body and if she'd seen anyone unusual lurking about the place anytime in the last couple of days. She had no answers for him.

Finally he was finished with her. Within another thirty minutes the body had been removed, and everyone was gone except Sam and Daniella, who once again sat at the kitchen table.

"The sheriff didn't act like you're one of his favorite people," Sam said.

"Five years ago my husband disappeared, and I not only made myself a nuisance to Jim, but at one point I called him an incompetent jerk who should be waiting tables instead of working investigations."

"Ouch. So, *is* he incompetent?" Sam asked.

She shrugged. "I don't know. I thought he was when I was trying to find my husband, but that was just my personal opinion. I know he's retiring at the end of the year, which will be a good thing."

"Macy said her daddy got lost." Sam leaned forward in his chair, his gaze intent as he gazed at her. "What happened to him?"

She could fall into those blue depths if she allowed herself. She reminded herself that even though he'd been a support, he was simply a guest who would be gone within two weeks.

"I wish I knew," she answered. As always, thoughts of Johnny brought with them a faint edge of grief and a whisper of unresolved anger. "Five years ago he left here to drive into town to get diapers for Macy and he never came back. At first I thought maybe he'd been involved in an accident, but when I called Jim nobody had reported anything like that. I called Jeff, Johnny's best friend, to see if he'd heard anything from him. He hadn't, but he made the rounds of all the bars and hangouts in town looking for Johnny."

How well she remembered that night. As the hours had worn on with no word from her husband she'd been frantic with worry, certain that something terrible had happened to the man she loved.

She swallowed hard to dislodge the lump that rose in the back of her throat. "When twenty-four hours had passed I went down to Jim's office and filed an official missing-persons report. Jim told me he'd check around but that it wasn't against the law for a husband to leave his wife."

"Were you and your husband having marital problems?"

It was a personal question but Daniella didn't take offense. Somehow, in the last couple of hours that passed with the investigation of a murder, between them had arisen a strange, false sense of intimacy.

"Johnny and I were high school sweethearts. We got married on the day I turned eighteen, and we shared the dream of buying this place and turning it into a successful bed-and-breakfast. We were married four years when I got pregnant with Macy. That same year my mother died, and we used the money from her life insurance policy to buy this place. Macy was two months old when we moved in, and for the next two months we painted and scrubbed and did everything we could to get this place ready to open." She realized she was rambling, telling him more than he'd asked for, but it seemed important that he know the details.

"Things were good," she continued. "We had the baby we wanted and were on our way to seeing our dream come true, and then he was just gone."

"Was there an official investigation into his disappearance?" Sam asked.

"Eventually, but he and his car were never found. For a long time I entertained all kinds of ideas. He'd been in an accident and had hit his head and suffered amnesia. He was kidnapped at gunpoint and was being held captive for some unknown reason. Jim thought that he'd just walked away from the responsibility of the business, the baby and me, but I couldn't imagine Johnny doing that. A year ago I finally decided to get a divorce on grounds of abandonment. And I'm sorry. I've bored you long enough."

She pushed back from the table, embarrassed that she'd spilled so much personal information to him. "Thank you for all your support tonight, and now back to your regular scheduled vacation plans." She stood and he did the same.

"If the sheriff needs to talk to you again and you want somebody there with you, just let me know," he said.

She smiled gratefully at him. "Thanks, but I just hope you can put all this behind you and enjoy the rest of your time here. But I would understand if you want to leave and stay someplace else." She froze as she saw her cordless phone on the counter. Suddenly she remembered the strange phone call she'd gotten earlier in the day.

"I'm not going anywhere for now. Daniella, is something wrong?" Sam took a step closer to her and once again she noticed the sexy scent of him.

"It's probably nothing," she said. "I just had a weird phone call this morning."

"Weird how?"

Once again she was struck not only by the rich color of his eyes but by the hard edge of intelligence that shone there. "It was an anonymous call. I didn't recognize the voice, but it sounded like he said 'for you' and then hung up." A cold chill walked up her spine. "But surely it didn't have anything to do with Samantha's death. That just doesn't make sense, does it?"

Sam held her gaze for a long moment. "Let's hope not," he finally said, but the answer did nothing to dispel the cold wind that blew through Daniella.

Chapter Three

For you.

The two words were the first thing that jumped into Sam's head when he opened his eyes the next morning. The sun was already up, and his first impulse was to jump out of bed. Then he reminded himself that he was on vacation. There was no reason to hurry out of the comfortable bed.

For you.

The phone call to Daniella bothered him and had kept him tossing and turning until nearly dawn. Several things that had happened the night before had kept sleep at bay.

Daniella's story of the disappearance of her husband had managed to touch the heart he'd thought had died years ago. It was a testament to her strength that she'd continued on here, making a success of this place all alone.

At least she didn't have to worry about the crime shutting her down. It was obvious that the bed-and-breakfast was merely the dumping site, and the murder had occurred elsewhere. The victim was from town, with no ties to the business where her body had been found.

They could all speculate on why the body had been dumped in this particular place, but at the moment it would be only speculation.

The other thing that had bothered him was the sheriff's attitude toward Daniella. Obviously he hadn't gotten over whatever past was between them. His attitude had bordered on rude, and Sam had a feeling the sheriff had a little bully in him. At least he'd agreed to provide patrols in the area.

Still, his mind kept returning to that damned phone call she'd received.

For you.

Had Daniella misunderstood what the caller had said? Was the phone call tied to the murder? And if so, then what did it have to do with Daniella? She'd said she didn't know Samantha that well, that they'd had no relationship to speak of.

When he had finally fallen asleep nightmares had tormented him. He dreamed of monsters, but they were familiar visions, part of the past he'd spent his adult life trying to forget.

He finally pulled himself out of bed and padded into the bathroom for a shower. As he started the water he reminded himself that he was on vacation, that none of this was his problem.

Minutes later, as he dried off, his thoughts once again turned to Daniella. He definitely had the hots for her. Even through the stress of the night before his senses had spun with her clean, floral scent. When he'd touched her even in the most simple way his heart had raced just a little faster and a surge of adrenaline had filled him.

As hard as she was to resist, he didn't intend to follow through on his attraction. He realized the last thing she needed in her life was a dead-hearted bastard nicknamed the Prince of Darkness. There had been enough darkness in her life. He didn't need to infect her with any of his own.

It was just after nine when he made his way down to the dining room. He knew he was too late for breakfast but was hoping to find some coffee.

The house was silent and the dining room empty, with no coffee urn set up. He followed the sound of clinking dishes into the kitchen, where he found Daniella standing with her back to him at the sink.

She was clad in a pair of denim shorts that cupped her sexy butt and showcased her shapely legs. Her pink tank top accentuated her light tan, and the burst of adrenaline he was determined not to feel surged up inside of him.

"Am I too late for coffee?" he asked, irritated at his immediate response to her.

She whirled around to face him, her cheeks instantly filling with color. "Oh, you startled me." She grabbed a towel from the counter and quickly dried her hands. "Have a seat and I'll pour you a cup." She pointed to the kitchen table, and as he slid into a chair she got a mug from the cabinet.

"It's quiet around here this morning," he said, once she'd poured his coffee.

"Matt is out, and Frank just left to take Macy on a play date with her best friend. Would you like some breakfast? I'd be happy to whip you up some eggs or something."

He shook his head and wrapped his fingers around the warm coffee mug. "No thanks, I'll just wait until lunch." What he wanted to do was take his coffee and leave the kitchen, escape from the warmth of her eyes when she gazed at him, from the scent of her that lingered in the air.

But before he could escape she poured herself a cup of coffee and joined him at the table. "I want to thank you again for last night." She reached up and tucked a strand of her shining blond hair behind a dainty ear. "Not only for supporting me when I talked to Jim, but also for listening to me ramble about Johnny and my past. I promise you I don't usually burden my guests like that."

"It wasn't a burden, and I know that nothing about last night was business as usual." He took a sip of his coffee and tried not to notice how soft, how silky, her hair looked, tried to ignore the impulse to reach out and tangle his fingers in the strands.

"You have a wife, Sam? Somebody significant in your life?"

Her question came out of left field and surprised him. "No, no wife, no girlfriend, no interest in having either," he replied. "I like being unattached. What about you?

You have a boyfriend? In the market for another marriage?" He wasn't sure why he asked; it wasn't like he cared.

"No boyfriend," she replied. "As far as getting married again, I think you need a boyfriend to even think about it."

"You and Jeff seem fairly close. Any romantic sparks there?"

She laughed, and the delightful sound of her laughter wrapped around the heart he professed he didn't own. "Jeff was best man at my wedding, and at that time he promised Johnny that if anything happened to him he'd be there for me. He's stayed true to his word. He's like a big brother to me, but there certainly isn't anything romantic between us."

Sam would have bet his badge that Jeff felt far more for Daniella than brotherly feelings. The night before at dinner, he'd seen it in the man's eyes each time Jeff had looked at Daniella.

"I'm not sure how I'd have kept it all together after Johnny disappeared if it wasn't for Jeff and Frank," she continued.

He knew he should get out of the kitchen, get away from her, but his body didn't seem to be listening to his head. "How did Frank come to work for you?"

"Frank worked with Johnny at a factory in town, and they were friends. The plant closed about the same time we bought this place. Frank knew there was a small caretaker cabin on the other side of the pond, and Johnny agreed to hire him as a handyman and let Frank live there. He's been with me ever since."

A knock on the door interrupted the conversation, and Sam breathed a sigh of relief as she got up from the table to answer it.

What in the hell was he doing sitting at the table chatting with her? Why did he find the shine of the sun on her hair so enchanting? The curve of her lips such a damned temptation?

Apparently he needed not only a vacation but a brain adjustment, as well. He definitely needed to get some distance from Daniella Butler, who made him think of rumpled bedsheets and sweet feminine curves and mindless, soul-searing sex.

He quickly drained his coffee mug and got up to carry it to the sink. He should be catching fish instead of fishing for information about a woman who he would never allow to matter to him.

He turned away from the sink and saw Daniella re-entering the room, followed closely by a grim-looking Sheriff Jim Thompson.

"Jim has some more questions for me," she said to Sam. The sparkle that had lit her eyes earlier was gone, replaced by dark worry. She sank down in a chair at the table, but both men remained standing.

"Several things have come up between last night and this morning that I find troubling," Jim said. He directed a harsh gaze at Daniella. "I think maybe you haven't been completely honest with me."

"About what?" Daniella looked shocked.

Jim waved a hand toward Sam, as if to dismiss him. "I don't think we need you here, Mr. Connelly."

Sam didn't like the way the sheriff stood too close to her chair, as if in an effort to intimidate her. He didn't know what exactly was going on, but he wasn't going to leave Daniella alone with the man.

"Consider my interest a professional one," he said. He pulled his wallet from his back pocket, opened it and laid it in the center of the table, his FBI identity card exposed.

He was aware of Daniella's look of surprise, but Jim looked none too happy at this new information. "This isn't an FBI matter," he said stiffly. "It's a local one and we handle our own."

"I understand that," Sam said smoothly. "But Daniella wants me here while you speak to her, and so I have no intention of leaving at the moment."

"The way I see it she doesn't need an FBI man, although before this is all over she might need a good defense attorney," Jim replied.

Daniella gasped. "Jim, dear God, what are you talking about?"

"I found out last night about Samantha's plans…plans that would have put her in direct competition with you," he said.

"What plans?" Daniella's face had gone pale, and Sam fought the impulse to step closer to her, to touch her shoulder or pull her into his arms for support.

He'd known her for only twenty-four hours, but his gut instinct told him there was no way in hell she had anything to do with the murder of Samantha Walker, and his gut was rarely wrong.

"Samantha was planning on opening her own bed-and-breakfast. For the last couple of weeks she's been going around town telling everyone the town wasn't big enough for two of you and she intended to be top dog."

Sam knew the shock on Daniella's face was genuine. "I…I didn't know," she finally managed to say. "I hadn't heard about her plans to open a bed-and-breakfast."

"She would have been a tough competitor. She had plenty of money, and I figure it wouldn't have been long before she put you right out of business," Jim replied.

"Surely you don't think I had anything to do with her murder?" Daniella jumped up out of her chair and faced the sheriff. "This is crazy. I had nothing to do with it. How could you even think such a thing?" She trembled with the force of her emotions, and her face paled even more.

"I'm sure the sheriff has other suspects," Sam said, as he stepped closer to her.

"There have to be other suspects," Daniella exclaimed. "Because I had nothing to do with this."

"I'm just at the beginning of this investigation," Jim said. "I just wanted to talk to you about this whole competing bed-and-breakfast thing."

"You'd better be talking to somebody else because you're wasting time talking to me," Daniella replied. "I didn't know about any plans Samantha had, and even if I did I wouldn't have killed her."

"I'll see myself out," Jim said. "I guess I don't have to tell you not to leave town." He didn't wait for a reply but left the kitchen, and a moment later the front door slammed shut.

Daniella looked at Sam, her beautiful eyes filled with tears. She looked fragile, like she might fly into a million pieces, and before Sam recognized his intent he stepped forward and drew her into his arms.

She leaned into him, a trembling mass of tantalizing curves. Her hair smelled like a floral-scented summer breeze and he instantly realized his mistake in holding her so close.

She buried her face in the front of his T-shirt and released a deep, tremulous sigh as he patted her back awkwardly and tried to pretend he wasn't aroused by her very nearness.

Finally she raised her head and looked up at him, her eyes dark with emotion. "I had nothing to do with this," she said, her voice a half whisper.

"I know." He dropped his arms from around her and took a step backward. Two words thundered in his brain.

For you.

For you.

He shoved his hands in his pockets as he held her gaze. "But I think it's possible somebody you know did have something to do with it." He didn't think it was possible for blue eyes to go so dark, but hers were nearly black as she returned his gaze.

"The phone call," she whispered, as if afraid to say

the words out loud. She reached out and took his hands in hers. "Oh, Sam, what am I going to do?"

She squeezed his hands, and he felt a sinking sensation in the pit of his stomach as he wondered how in the hell he was going to keep himself uninvolved from this crime and from this woman.

THIS WAS HER FAVORITE time of the day, when dinner was finished and the dishes were done and Daniella had a little downtime to enjoy.

As the day had worn on Daniella had almost managed to convince herself that she'd misunderstood the words the anonymous caller had said to her.

The voice had been strange and she'd had to strain to hear what he'd said. It was possible he'd only said something that sounded like *for you*.

She now sat on the front porch and watched Macy doing cartwheels across the lawn. The sun rode low in the sky, and the heat of the day had eased to a pleasant temperature, but her mind was far away from her daughter's acrobatic skills and the weather.

She'd called Jim earlier in the day to tell him about the phone call, and as she'd explained it to him she'd thought she'd heard the sound of nails being driven into her coffin.

How could Jim believe that she had anything to do with Samantha's murder? And how could she possibly believe that anyone close to her was capable of such a thing? It was too awful to even consider.

Most of the afternoon she'd thought about the

supportive people in her life, and there was no way she could imagine any of them doing something so heinous. She'd known Frank and Jeff for years, and they'd never shown any hint that they were capable of such violence.

She smelled him before she saw him, that crisp, clean scent that tightened something in the pit of her stomach. She turned her head and smiled as Sam stepped out on the porch.

"How are you doing?" he asked, as he eased down into the wicker chair next to hers.

"Okay. I've spent most of the day thinking about everything, about who might be responsible for Samantha's murder."

"Did you come up with any answers?"

"No, but I can tell you this—Samantha wasn't a popular woman in town. She had more money than she knew what to do with and never let anyone forget it. I hate to speak ill of the dead, but Samantha was a petty, mean woman. Over the last couple of years I've heard rumors about all kinds of businesses she intended to open—a beauty shop, a restaurant and an upscale boutique—but none of them ever materialized. I wouldn't have worried if I'd heard that she was on a bed-and-breakfast kick. Anyone who knew Samantha knew she was big on talk and never followed through."

"Then Jim has his hands full with the investigation," Sam replied. "Hopefully he's up to the job."

"Hopefully he is, because I don't want to go to jail for something I had nothing to do with."

"I wouldn't let that happen," he said gruffly.

His words created a ball of warmth in her stomach, a warmth she hadn't felt for a very long time. *Watch out,* she told herself. *He's just a guest and nothing more.*

"Mr. Sam!" Macy yelled. "Watch this!" She did a series of cartwheels and then stood proudly, waiting for his response.

"That's great," he said, as if surprised that she would want his approval.

Macy ran up to the porch. "I didn't get to show you my princess walk last night, so I'll do it now."

Before he or Daniella could respond, Macy tore into the house where Daniella knew she was fetching her crown.

"She has a lot of energy," Sam said.

Daniella laughed. "That's probably the understatement of the century. She's opinionated and maybe more than a little bit spoiled, but she really is a good kid. She has a tremendous heart and she loves people."

At that moment the door opened and Macy pranced out, her glittery crown firmly in place on top of her head. "Are you ready, Mr. Sam?"

"I think I'm ready as I'll ever be," he replied.

Macy ran to the far end of the porch. "This is my official princess walk." The walk was less princess and more fairy sprite as she danced her way back to them.

"I do believe that was the finest princess walk I've ever seen," Sam said when she'd finished.

Daniella flashed him a grateful smile and then looked at her daughter. "And now it's time for the princess to go take a bath. It's not nice for a princess to smell like a day of grit and grime."

Macy looked at Sam. "And maybe tomorrow I can have a princess tea party, and you can come and be my guest of honor."

"No time for tea parties tomorrow," Daniella said. "I have new guests arriving, and besides, Mr. Sam has other things to do."

"Okay, then we'll have a tea party another day," Macy said agreeably. She disappeared into the house to get ready for her bath and Daniella once again turned to look at Sam.

"I'm sorry, she seems to have taken a liking to you."

He offered her a small smile and gazed out in the distance. "Guess there's no accounting for taste."

No, there was no accounting for taste, she mentally agreed. And whatever had bitten her daughter when it came to Sam Connelly had bitten Daniella just a little bit, as well.

"How long have you been an FBI agent?" she asked, as she relaxed against the back of the wicker chair.

He turned back to look at her, and as always she found the blue of his eyes intoxicating. "I joined the agency when I was twenty-two, fresh out of college and eager to catch the bad guys."

"What exactly is it that you do?" Usually with guests she kept her distance, didn't try to find out personal details about them except what they liked to eat and how they liked their rooms kept. But, she wanted to know more about this man with his eyes that alternately filled with humor and darkened with demons. Besides, talking about him was far better than thinking about the horror show her life had become over the last twenty-four hours.

"I'm a profiler," he replied.

"So you profile killers?" she asked with interest.

"Actually, profiling starts with us looking closely at the victims of crimes. We learn everything we can about them and that gives us an idea of the killer. Then we try to get into the head of the person who committed the crime. We try to figure out what drives them, what wants or needs they have and finally what weakness they might possess that would allow us to catch them."

"Must be fascinating."

"It is," he agreed. "It's also intense and all-consuming and takes me to some very dark places."

"Your parents must be very proud of you." She noticed the tension that had begun to radiate from him as he spoke of his work.

"My parents are dead." His tone was flat, emotionless.

"Oh, I'm sorry."

He shrugged. "It was a long time ago."

An awkward silence fell between them as he once again directed his gaze into the distance. Dusk was falling quickly, layering the dark shadows of approaching night all around. She knew she should go inside. She had a ton of things to do for the new arrivals the next day, but she was reluctant to leave the porch, to leave Sam.

"Bachelor Moon," he said, breaking the silence. "It's kind of an odd name. How did it come about?"

She smiled. "Legend has it that Larry Bridges, our founding father, was standing in the center square one evening beneath a full moon. Larry was a confirmed bachelor, but that night a mysterious, beautiful woman appeared, and within six months they were married. He named the town Bachelor Moon. Legend has it that when a single man stands in that particular place in the town square beneath a full moon he will be wed within six months. There's even a statue denoting the specific place to stand."

"And I assume this legend brings its fair share of tourists to the area?"

She smiled. "That's what legends are for." Once again she thought that she should go inside, that Macy needed her bath so she could be tucked into bed.

But she was reluctant to leave. The night air was sweetly scented and pleasant, and there was no question that sitting so close to Sam had created a pleasant buzz through her veins.

"It must have been tough after your husband disappeared to stay here and make the business work," he said. His eyes glittered in the semidarkness.

"After a month had passed I thought about just packing up and putting the place back on the market and walking away. But then I worried that if Johnny came back he wouldn't know where to find us. As the months went by I got angry and decided if Johnny had willfully walked away from us, then I was going to make this the best damned bed-and-breakfast to prove to him that I could."

"Prove to him or prove to yourself?"

She smiled thoughtfully. "Maybe a little of both. I'm comfortable with where I am and who I've become over the last five years. I've made peace with the fact that Johnny is gone forever and I'm moving along with my life. And speaking of moving on with my life, I'd better get back inside."

She stood and he got up at the same time. As they both stepped in the direction of the door they were suddenly face-to-face, intimately close.

Their gazes locked, and then his slowly slid down to her lips and she knew he wanted to kiss her. And as crazy as it seemed, she wanted that, too.

Her breath caught in her throat, and she suddenly ached with the need to feel his mouth on hers and to mold herself against his body. She wanted his strong arms to wrap her up so tight she couldn't think about murder or Johnny's disappearance, but only about him.

The tension between them snapped as he stepped back from her and gestured her to go before him through the door. Disappointment fluttered through her, and she shook her head to admonish herself. "You go on. I've got a few things to do out here on the porch."

He hesitated a moment, then with a murmured good-night he went inside. When he disappeared she released a tremulous sigh. What was she thinking? Wanting a kiss from a guest?

She must have been more unsettled than she thought about the murder and Jim's suspicions of her. She took a moment to arrange the chairs on the porch, then stood and stared out into the darkness of night.

Sam.

The man shook her up almost as much as the murder and Jim's ridiculous suspicions of her. Sam had thought about kissing her. She'd seen it in his eyes. He'd wanted to kiss her. The thought shot a little thrill up her spine. It had been a very long time since she'd seen that in a man's eyes, since she'd wanted a kiss from any man.

As she remained looking out at the darkness a new chill suddenly slithered up her spine. The base of her scalp tingled with a prickly feeling, and she had the inexplicable feeling that somebody was watching her. She narrowed her eyes and tried to pierce the deep veil of night. Was somebody out there in the dark? Had Samantha's killer returned?

"Silly fool," she muttered beneath her breath. As Macy would say, monsters had no power when there were princesses present.

Daniella was jumping at shadows, feeling the presence of an imaginary boogeyman. What had happened to Samantha had nothing to do with her. She was safe here. Comforted by her own thoughts, she turned and went into the house.

THE MOMENT SHE DISAPPEARED from his sight, he leaned back against the large tree trunk and drew a deep, steadying breath.

Daniella.

Daniella.

Her name was a song in his heart, a burn in the depths of his soul.

She didn't know it yet, but she belonged to him. It was written on the face of the Bachelor Moon, roaring on the wind of fate, emblazoned on his heart.

He loved her. And now he'd killed for her. There was no way he could let that bitch Samantha run around town and badmouth Daniella and her business.

So far he'd been patient…so damned patient.

But his patience was wearing thin, his need to claim her becoming an overwhelming force. Soon, he promised himself. Soon he would make his move, claim her and her daughter. All he had to do was finish his work on their new home, a secret place where he could keep them with him through eternity.

Chapter Four

He stood in the kitchen, a seething mass of sick energy, the shotgun a terrifying extension of his hairy arm. Eyes wild, sweat dripping from his forehead, he embodied every nightmare Sam had ever had of a monster.

Sam's mother stood against the kitchen cabinets, her pretty face blanched of color, her entire body trembling uncontrollably. "Sam," she whispered, as he walked into the room.

Sam carefully set his book bag on the floor. "What's going on, Dad?"

"I'm going to kill your mother." His calm, matter-of-fact tone was even more terrifying than if he'd screamed the words. "And then I'm gonna kill you."

Before Sam could properly process anything the shotgun boomed and his mother crumpled to the floor. In a fog of shock, he watched as the shotgun swung in his direction.

"No!" He turned to run.

Sam sat straight up in bed, his breaths coming in deep gasps and his body coated with a sheen of sweat. Adrenaline surged inside him, the fight-or-flight response to danger.

His heart finally slowed to a more normal beat and he dragged a hand across his jawline as he tried to dispel the horrible memories.

Monsters. His father had been the first in his life, but certainly not the last. He stumbled from the bed, feeling half-drunk with the aftereffects of the nightmare still burning inside his brain.

After a long hot shower he dressed in a pair of jeans and a navy, short-sleeved, ribbed pullover. He wasn't going to hang around the bed-and-breakfast today, but rather he intended to spend some time in town.

It had been two days since he'd almost kissed Daniella on the front porch, and for the past two days he'd kept his distance from her. It had been relatively easy with the onslaught of new guests. He'd fished, he'd napped and he'd placed himself wherever Daniella wasn't at the moment.

Today was Sunday, the day that only breakfast was offered, the day that the weekend guests would be leaving. He'd decided he'd drive into town and hang out, maybe listen to some of the local gossip and see if he could hear what people were saying, were thinking, about Samantha Walker's murder.

They hadn't seen any more of the sheriff, but that didn't mean it was all over where Daniella was concerned. Sam couldn't control the vague, bad feeling he had about the whole situation. Maybe a day in the quaint town of Bachelor Moon would rectify the faint anxiety that bubbled just beneath the surface.

Of course the first person he saw as he came down the stairs was Daniella. Her smile sizzled through his veins as he nodded a good morning.

"Breakfast is ready in the dining room," she said.

"Actually, I thought I'd head into town this morning, taste a little of the local flavor," he replied.

"If you decide to eat at Mama's Café be sure to have Tina wait on you. She's my best friend and she'll take good care of you."

He nodded, eager to get away from her. She looked so pretty in a blue sundress that enhanced her eyes and showcased her curves. She was sweet temptation in the flesh.

"Will you be back for dinner? Although officially I don't cook anything, you paid for meals so I'd be happy to have something ready for you," she said.

"Don't worry about it. I'll take care of myself for the day." He could hear the sounds of the guests in the dining room, all of whom would be checking out after breakfast. "I'll see you later."

He escaped out the front door, away from her scent, from the smile that made him want to wrap her in his arms and carry her to his bed.

His attraction to Daniella was obviously one of those chemistry things that he'd heard about, something he'd never experienced before now. But just because he felt it didn't mean he intended to follow through on it.

It was almost nine o'clock when he pulled into Bachelor Moon proper. It was a small town with a small-town feel. A variety of businesses lined the city block, with the town hall and a park in the center. Magnolia trees provided not only welcome shade but also beauty. Shop doors were open despite the growing heat and humidity, as if inviting everyone to pass into their depths.

He parked in front of Mama's Café and got out of the car. The air drifting out of the door from the café was redolent with the scents of frying bacon, yeasty rolls and sautéed onions. It set his mouth watering, but he had already decided to skip breakfast and eat lunch at the café.

He headed in the direction of the city square, deciding to check out the place where the legend of Bachelor Moon had begun. It was a gorgeous day, and it felt good for him to stretch his legs a bit after several days of sitting in a chair on the dock.

As he crossed the street he noticed the sheriff's office on the other side of the town square. He thought about stopping in and checking on the progress of the investigation into Samantha's murder, but then reminded himself that it was really none of his business.

It was easy to find the legend place. A statue of a man stood before the town hall, and in his hand was a stone tablet that read:

He who stands here beneath a bachelor moon,
If your heart is open you will find love soon.

You might think this is silly local lore,
But the magic of the moon brings love forever
more.

At least he didn't have to worry about falling victim
to the magic of the moon. The next full moon was in
two weeks and he'd be long gone by then, back to work
in Kansas City.

Spying a nearby bench, he sat and raised his face to
the sun. If he was smart he'd go back to the bed-and-
breakfast, pack his bags and head back to Kansas City
now, before he got sucked into the drama of a local
murder, before he got sucked into the charming town
of Bachelor Moon and Daniella Butler.

He was still seated there minutes later when he saw
Jim Thompson leaving the sheriff's office. He stood and
knew the moment Jim saw him. The lawman's shoulders
stiffened and he drew himself up, as if it were possible
for him to make himself as tall as Sam's six feet.

He strode across the square toward Sam. "Taking in
some of the local sights, Mr. Connelly—or should I say
Special Agent Connelly?"

"Sam will do, and yes, I decided to check out the
town this morning."

"It's a nice place, but I imagine it's pretty slow-paced
for somebody like you."

"To be honest, I'm really enjoying the slower pace.
Daniella mentioned you were going to retire at the end
of the year. This looks like it would be a great place to
do it," Sam said.

"Actually my wife has her heart set on some retirement village in Florida." Jim took a step backward. "But I hope you enjoy your visit here."

"Before you go, how is the investigation into the murder progressing?" Sam wanted to kick himself for asking. Once a profiler, always a profiler, he thought wryly.

Jim's features tightened as if he wasn't happy with the question. "Daniella Butler is still my number one suspect. Oh, I know she didn't do the deed herself, but we're checking into a hired-killer situation."

Sam wanted to laugh out loud at the very idea of Daniella hiring somebody to murder Samantha, but it wasn't funny that Jim entertained such a scenario.

"You know that's crazy," he said. "I certainly hope there isn't a rush to judgment in this case. The way I hear it, Samantha Walker was the kind of woman who might have had lots of enemies."

"I've been the law around these parts for almost twenty years," Jim said with more than a touch of indignation. "I reckon I can get this right without any help. I didn't say Daniella was my only suspect. You just enjoy your visit here in Bachelor Moon and leave this all to me." He didn't wait for Sam's reply, but turned on his heel and stalked away.

Sam sank back to the bench, unsatisfied with the brief conversation. Despite what Jim had said, he hoped like hell Jim wasn't so focused on Daniella that he was ignoring other potential suspects.

Not my concern, he reminded himself. In just over a

week he'd be gone. Daniella and the charming town of Bachelor Moon would be just a distant memory.

He sat for a few more minutes enjoying the sun, then got up and wandered down the street. He drifted into a variety of shops, making small talk with the locals and getting a feel for some of the people who lived there.

It was a friendly town. People he passed smiled or paused to exchange pleasantries. It didn't take long for him to learn that nobody seemed to have much respect for Jim Thompson, nobody appeared to be in mourning for Samantha Walker, and Daniella and Macy were favorites among the people he talked to.

By the time twelve-thirty came he was starving. He made his way back to Mama's Café, where he immediately identified the Tina whom Daniella had spoken of earlier. It was easy to identify her because she was about Daniella's age and she wore a name tag.

She was a cute blonde with a ready smile and eyes the color of a chocolate bar. She was working the long counter where displays of pastries sat next to a stack of morning papers.

Sam slid onto an empty stool, grateful to find one in the busy place. Almost all the tables were filled, and it was obvious Mama's was one of the most popular places in town at mealtimes.

Tina approached him, a smile of welcome on her pretty face as she slapped a menu down before him. "How are you doing? Our lunch special today is Cajun shrimp with coleslaw and cheese biscuits. Can I get you something to drink to start you off?"

"A tall glass of iced tea would be great," he replied.

"Coming right up."

As she left to get his drink, he glanced around the café. It certainly wasn't the ambiance that made this place popular. The cutlery and dinnerware was mismatched and some of the water glasses looked suspiciously like old jelly jars. The decor was a mishmash of colors and styles, as if the decorator suffered from multiple personality disorder.

But laughter rang out from many of the tables along with the easy conversation of people comfortable not only with each other but with their surroundings.

"Here you go," Tina said, as she returned with his iced tea. "Have you decided what to order?"

"I'll take that special."

"You won't be disappointed. Mama's Cajun shrimp is delicious." As she disappeared into the back kitchen, Sam leaned against the counter and took a drink of the tea.

As he waited for his meal to arrive his thoughts filled with Daniella and that dangerous moment on the porch when he'd wanted to kiss her.

Nothing good could come from kissing Daniella Butler. After being around her for almost a week he knew that she wasn't the type of woman to indulge in a hot temporary encounter with one of her guests. And he certainly wasn't the kind of man who would be interested in sticking around with any woman.

Sam liked women, but only on his terms, and that meant temporary. He wouldn't allow any of them close enough to get into his heart. A crash from the kitchen startled him and suddenly he remembered the dream he'd had the night before, the dream of the gunshot that had changed his life.

It was a memory of early life that burned inside him, that made him fear that a monster slept in his soul, a monster that might one day awaken and wreak destruction.

He was his father's son, and he spent every day of his life afraid of what might rest inside him, afraid that if he didn't keep a tight rein on his emotions, the monster would leap free and destroy anyone he cared about. It was easier not to care, to never allow anyone to get close.

Tina returning with his meal halted the disturbing thoughts. "You visiting the area or just passing through?" she asked as she placed the oversize plate before him.

"I'm staying out at Daniella's."

Tina smiled. "Daniella is the best, isn't she? She and I have been best friends since the third grade."

"It's a shame about her husband."

Tina's eyebrows rose. "She told you about Johnny? She almost never talks about him anymore."

He nodded. "It's hard to believe a man would run off from a woman like her."

"There are some here in town that think he ran off. I don't know what happened to him, but I'll never believe he left her," she exclaimed. "We all hung out together through high school, Daniella and Johnny, me and Matt and Jeff and his girlfriend."

"Matt?"

"Matt Rader. He's living out at Daniella's right now while his house is being built." Tina looked down the counter, obviously checking to see if she was needed anywhere else.

"I didn't realize Matt was a local," Sam replied.

She looked back at him. "He's local, although after college he moved to Shreveport and got married. His wife passed away about eight months ago, and he moved back here to start again. I think maybe he's developed a little crush on Daniella."

"Did you know Samantha Walker?"

Tina nodded and frowned. "A nasty piece of work, if you ask me. I talked briefly to Daniella on the phone the day after Samantha was found. She was pretty shook up about the whole thing." She waved to one of the other diners down at the opposite end of the counter. "Gotta run. Enjoy your meal."

As she left Sam stared down at his plate, but his thoughts were a churning mess of suppositions, and he realized that no matter his desire to the contrary, he was slowly being sucked into the mystery of Samantha Walker's murder.

IT HAD BEEN A GOOD DAY. Sunday afternoons when the guests left were always days when Daniella focused on special time with Macy. With Frank holding the fort at the bed-and-breakfast, she always tried to take Macy out and away from the house for some mommy-daughter time.

Today they'd driven into the slightly bigger neighboring town of Baker's Bluff and had seen the newest Disney movie. Afterward they had eaten at a pizza place and were now in the car heading home.

"It was a fun day," Macy said.

"Yes, it was, but I always enjoy spending free time with my favorite girl," Daniella replied. She turned on her headlights against the encroaching dusk.

"Do you think Daddy will ever, ever get found?"

Macy's question pierced through Daniella's heart. It was just in the last year that Macy was asking more and more questions about the father she'd never known.

A million answers swept through Daniella's head as the need to somehow make her daughter happy filled her soul. But, ultimately she knew the truth was what Macy needed.

"No, honey. I don't think Daddy will ever be found," she finally replied.

"I didn't think so," Macy replied, as if unsurprised by the answer. "I think we need to look for a new daddy. I think Mr. Sam would make a good new daddy."

Even the simple sound of his name shot a rivulet of warmth through Daniella. "Honey, Mr. Sam is just a guest. He's going to be leaving in another week."

"But maybe I could make him stay," Macy countered. "He thought I had the best princess walk and he's nice and he smells good and I think I could make him love me if I tried really hard."

Daniella's heart broke a little bit at her daughter's

words and she cursed Johnny Butler, not for leaving her but for walking away from Macy.

"Macy, honey, Mr. Sam isn't going to be a new daddy, so you might as well get that thought out of your head." Daniella turned down the long, tree-lined lane that led to the bed-and-breakfast. "Maybe someday you'll have a new daddy, but for now we just have to be happy with each other."

Macy didn't reply, and it made Daniella wonder what was going on in her amazing little brain. As they pulled up in front of the house her heart did a little dance as she saw Sam seated on the front porch.

"There's Mr. Sam," Macy exclaimed, sitting up taller in her seat.

"I don't want you bothering him with this daddy stuff," Daniella warned, as she pulled the car to a halt. "Did you hear me, Macy Marie?"

"Okay. Look, the fireflies are out. Can I catch some before bedtime?"

Daniella sighed in relief. "Go get your jar. You have about thirty minutes before bath time."

Before Daniella could get her seat belt off and out of the car, Macy was out and in the house to get her bug-catching jar.

"You look relaxed," she said to Sam, as she walked up the stairs to the porch.

He smiled. "I am. This is the best seat in the house for watching the sun go down."

"Did you enjoy your visit in town?" She sat in the chair next to his even though she knew the smartest thing she could do was stay as far away from him as possible. He made her think of things she shouldn't, want things she knew she couldn't have with him.

"I did. It's a charming town and everyone seemed friendly. I had lunch at Mama's and met your friend, Tina."

"She's great. And it's a wonderful town."

At that moment Macy raced outside, her neon green bug jar in her hand. "Mr. Sam, I'm going to collect some fireflies. I don't kill them or pull out their lights or anything like that. I just catch them and watch them for a while and then I let them go. I think they're the prettiest bug God ever made." She didn't wait for his reply but raced off the porch.

"Everyone speaks very highly of you and Macy seems to be a favorite," he said. His eyes glowed like something wild in the deepening darkness.

She smiled as she watched Macy racing across the lawn in pursuit of a lightning bug. "Macy can be a little charmer if she wants, but she also can be the most stubborn, sassy little girl I've ever met." She slid him a sideways glance. "Ever wanted children?"

"Never." He seemed to blurt out the word with more force than necessary. He smiled as if to temper his reply, but she saw the tension that knotted his jaw. "I always figured I'd screw up the dad thing. My old man wasn't exactly a good role model."

She waited for him to say something more on the subject, but instead he focused his attention on Macy and fell silent. She wanted to ask him more, wanted to know about where he came from, what kind of life he'd had, why he'd chosen to go through life alone. But she had no right to pry, she reminded herself. He was just a guest and would be gone all too soon.

"I didn't realize Matt was from here," he said, breaking the silence that had begun to feel oppressive.

"Born and raised here. He and Tina were quite an item before he moved to Shreveport. He broke her heart when he left. Everyone just assumed when he came back to town that he and Tina would pick up where they left off. She's divorced, he's widowed, it just seemed natural, but it hasn't happened."

"Tina thinks maybe Matt has a thing for you."

She looked at him in surprise. "She said that?" She laughed and shook her head. "Matt's just staying here while his house is being built. He should be out of here in a couple of weeks or so. If I was having a thing with everyone some of the people in town thought I was, I'd be the most sexually sated woman in the universe."

"And instead?" His gaze held hers with an intensity that captured her breath in her chest and made her wonder if she would ever breathe again.

"And instead if I thought about it long enough I'd admit that I'm lonely." She felt the warmth of the blush that swept over her cheeks.

Still his gaze held hers and she knew she should look away but she couldn't. A palpable tension simmered between them, a tension she hadn't felt for years but recognized as sweet, hot desire.

"You look like a woman who needs to be kissed."

His voice was low and husky and swept over her like a caress.

"Mr. Sam, look how many I caught!" Macy raced up on the porch, breaking the moment between Daniella and Sam.

Macy sidled up next to him and held out the jar that sparkled with the flashing lights of a dozen fireflies. She threw an arm around Sam's shoulder and leaned into him. "Aren't they pretty?"

He looked stunned by the easy way Macy clung to him. "They're really pretty," he replied.

Macy smiled at him. "And you like me, Mr. Sam, don't you?"

Uh-oh, Daniella thought. Apparently Macy hadn't listened to their discussion in the car. "Macy," she said in her best mom warning voice.

"Of course I like you," Sam replied.

"I thought so," Macy exclaimed. She leaned up and gave him a kiss on the cheek, then stepped away from him. Sam still wore a look of stunned surprise.

Daniella stood, more than a little bit irritated with her darling daughter. "Time to go inside, Macy."

"Okay, I just have to let them go." Macy unscrewed the lid of her jar and released the lightning bugs. "Goodbye, lightning bugs. I'll see you another time. Good night, Mr. Sam. I'll see you tomorrow."

An hour later Daniella sat at the kitchen table sipping a cup of hot tea. Bedtime kisses with Macy had included a mini lecture about not bothering the guests, but she had a feeling her words had gone right through Macy's head.

Macy was going to get her little heart broken if she thought there was a chance that Sam Connelly might become her new daddy.

Daniella stirred a spoonful of sugar into her tea and gave a little shake of her head. She'd never seen Macy act this way with any other male guest. She was obviously more hungry for a male role model in her life than Daniella had realized.

Sam Connelly definitely stirred a hunger in Daniella. Warmth swept through her as she thought of those moments earlier on the porch. He'd looked like he wanted to kiss her and despite all the reasons why it wasn't a good idea, she wished he had.

She hadn't lied when she'd told him she was lonely. When Johnny had first disappeared there hadn't been time for loneliness. Not only had she spent all her energy on trying to find out what had happened to him, she'd also needed to finish the work on the bed-and-breakfast so she could get some income streaming into the household.

In the past year she'd noticed the loneliness creeping steadily into her life. She'd awaken in the mornings alone in her bed and wish there was a warm male body to spoon against hers.

There were times she sat at this very table and wished there was somebody seated across from her, somebody with whom she could share the little nothings of her day.

She missed having somebody to watch the sunset with her, to hold her close on a stormy night.

A knock on the back door startled her and she looked up to see Jeff standing there. She got up and hurriedly unlocked the door to allow him inside.

"Hey, stranger," she greeted him. "I was wondering what happened to you over the last couple of days." She hadn't heard from Jeff since the night that Samantha's body had been found, when he'd eaten dinner with them.

"I had a conference to attend in Denver. I just got back this afternoon and heard about Samantha." He kissed her on the temple and then sat in the chair next to where she'd been sitting. "How are you doing?"

She returned to her chair. "Okay, despite the fact that Jim Thompson has me number one on his list of suspects." She smiled at the man who had been her husband's best friend, a man who had proven his friendship to her over the years since Johnny's disappearance. "I'm fine, really."

"I spoke to Jim before coming over here. That man shouldn't hold the office he does," Jeff scoffed. "Now he's wondering if maybe you make a habit of getting rid of people who are in your way." He shook his head. "He's thinks it's possible you killed Johnny and stashed his body somewhere it would never be found."

"Oh, for God's sake," Daniella exclaimed. The whole thing was too ludicrous to take seriously.

Jeff reached across the table and covered her hand with his. "Don't worry, I'm not going to let him railroad you. In fact, I think maybe it would be best that if Jim wants to question you again you direct him to me."

Jeff was one of two criminal defense lawyers in the area, and the fact that he thought she might need him was daunting. She pulled her hand from beneath his and leaned back in her chair. "Do you really think I'm in danger of being arrested?"

"No. I think Jim is blowing steam because he doesn't have any other leads. But I still think it best if you have as little contact with him as possible. We both know you aren't one of his favorite people."

"That's an understatement," she replied drily.

"I just wanted to stop by and see how you were doing, if there was anything you needed."

"I'm fine," she assured him. Jeff was a nice man, and Daniella suspected he wouldn't mind being more than friends to her. But it was never going to happen. She felt no sparks with him, nothing remotely romantic. "Go home, Jeff. You look tired."

"I am," he admitted, and raked a hand through his hair. "Conferences used to be about meetings, but this one was more about drinks in the bar and late nights." He stood and she did, as well.

"I appreciate you stopping by," she said, as they walked back to the door.

"Whatever you need, whenever you need it, you know I'm here for you," he replied. For a moment he gazed at her as if he wanted to say something more.

"Good night, Jeff," she said quickly, and opened the door.

"'Night, Daniella," he finally replied.

As he went out into the night she locked the door behind him and returned to her chair at the table. It was a shame she didn't feel anything romantic toward Jeff. He was a good man who would have made a good, supportive partner in life.

But he didn't excite her; he didn't make her heart leap when she saw him. The last thing she wanted was for him to speak of anything he might feel for her and ruin the easy friendship between them.

She finished her cup of tea, then carried the cup and saucer to the sink. She wished Jeff would find a wonderful woman and get married. He deserved to be happy, but she knew in her heart she would never be part of that happiness for him.

After placing her dishes in the dishwasher she turned around and gasped as she saw Sam standing in the doorway. Instantly her heart did a crazy leap. "You seem to make it a habit to startle me," she said.

"Sorry." He stepped into the kitchen, bringing with him a palpitating energy.

He was shirtless, and his dark hair was slightly tousled, as if he'd been in bed and for some reason decided to get up and had simply pulled on a pair of jeans. He was lean but his chest was well muscled, and the gleam in his eyes was every bit as hot as his body.

Daniella's mouth went dry as she remained frozen in place. She swallowed hard, trying to get her bearings. "Is there something you need?" she managed to say.

"Yeah, there is." He walked toward her with slow,

deliberate steps, his gaze never wavering from her. The closer he came to her the more her blood heated, finally reaching the sizzle-and-boil stage as he stood mere inches from her.

"I need that kiss we talked about earlier." His husky voice was filled with a need that nearly buckled her knees.

Daniella knew the difference between right and wrong, and she'd always told herself that it was wrong to get involved in any way with her guests, but at the moment she didn't care; she wanted to be wrong.

She didn't answer him, she simply leaned forward and raised her head to invite his kiss. She'd expected something simple, something light, but when he reached a hand up to cup the back of her head and pulled her tight against his bare chest, she knew this kiss wasn't going to be anything remotely resembling simple.

His mouth took hers with fiery intent, blazing a flame of desire in her that drove any other thought straight out of her head. She raised her arms around his neck, loving the feel of his warm, bare skin beneath her fingers.

When his tongue touched her bottom lip she was ready for him to deepen the kiss, and she opened her mouth and lost herself in him.

Their tongues swirled together in a sensual dance as his fingers tangled in her hair and his other hand slid slowly down her back. Against the strength of his body she felt warm and safe, even as the mastery of the kiss made her feel decidedly unsafe.

One hand remained at the back of her head while

the other stroked fire down her back, coming to rest on her waist. She used both her hands to caress his broad back, loving the feel of sinewy muscle just beneath the skin.

All too quickly he stopped. He dropped his hands to his sides and stepped back from her. His chest rose and fell in a rhythm that let her know he was as breathless as she, and his eyes nearly burned her with their intensity.

"Good night, Daniella." He turned on his heel and left her there, wanting more of him.

She released a tremulous breath and raised a hand to touch her lips. She still felt the imprint of his there, a sweet burn that tingled down to her toes.

As she left the kitchen and headed toward her bedroom she realized that Macy's heart might not be the only one broken when Sam Connelly went home.

HE LEANED AGAINST THE tree where Samantha Walker's body had been found and balled his hands into fists as a rage burned hot in his veins.

Kissing.

He'd seen them kissing, and the rage inside him welled up, tasting hot and bitter in his mouth.

She belonged to him, not to some guest who was here today and gone tomorrow. What was she thinking, letting that man put his mouth on hers, allowing him to pull her so close against him?

In all the years since her husband's disappearance he hadn't worried about her getting involved with another man. She'd been a devoted mother, an overworked business owner who hadn't taken time for a personal life.

He should kill Sam Connelly for putting his hands on her, for encroaching on property that wasn't his. He should kill him, but he wouldn't. Sam was an FBI agent, and his murder or disappearance would create more problems that it was worth, bring more attention than he wanted at the moment.

No, he wouldn't kill Sam Connelly, but it was time to take action. The disappearance of Daniella and Macy would also bring attention to the area, but nobody would ever find them and nobody would ever suspect him.

Once he had them he would begin a double life, going about his business as he always had but also spending his spare time with his new family. Eventually Daniella and Macy would love him, would realize they were a family and belonged together.

Yes, it was time he claimed what was his, time he claimed the woman he knew would make his perfect wife and the little girl who was his perfect daughter.

Chapter Five

Sam crept down the stairs as quiet as a shadow. Dawn hadn't even begun to lighten the eastern skies, but he'd awakened and had felt the need to escape the confines of his room.

He'd been a damned fool to kiss her. He'd gone out of his way to find her in the kitchen just so that he could take her in his arms and taste her mouth.

Fool.

He reached the bottom of the staircase and paused, listening for any noise to indicate that anyone else was awake in the house.

Silence. It was even too early for the woman of the house to be awake. That was fine with him. He needed a little alone time to get control of himself and his emotions where Daniella was concerned.

He unlocked the front door and stepped out on the porch. The early morning air was humid but relatively pleasant. It was still too dark to see much of anything, but he went to the railing and stood facing outward, and drew in several deep, cleansing breaths of air.

It wasn't just Daniella getting to him; it was Macy, as

well. When she'd leaned against him the night before, bringing with her the scent of innocence and childhood, it was as if a laser beam of light had pierced through the darkness inside him. And when she'd kissed his cheek, he'd had a fleeting thought that maybe it wouldn't be so bad to have a family.

Macy and Daniella were filling his head with crazy thoughts and he had to get control of himself. He remained standing at the railing until dawn began to break, streaking the sky with shades of pink and gold.

The official beginning of the day was marked by the rumble of a panel truck coming up the driveway. The side of the truck read: Ray's Laundry and Dry Cleaning Service. The truck disappeared around the side of the house, obviously making a delivery to the back door, and that meant Daniella was probably up and around.

Still he was reluctant to go back inside, maybe because he wanted to so badly. He wanted to see her smiling face, smell the scent of her that was evocative of sweet flowers and summer nights.

He turned away from the railing, deciding to sit for a little while longer before heading back inside. He frowned as he saw that one of the wicker chairs was already filled. A baby doll in a box tied with a bright pink bow sat next to a small floral arrangement of pink carnations. They had obviously been left by somebody for Macy and Daniella.

He picked them both up and went into the house where the scent of fresh-brewed coffee filled the air.

He heard her in the kitchen, apparently talking to the delivery man.

He set the items on the sideboard in the dining room and then went into the kitchen where Daniella was talking to a middle-aged man with oversized ears.

Her hair shone like spun gold in the first stirs of morning light, and he remembered how silky it had felt against his skin as he'd tangled his fingers in it. He consciously tried to will the remembered sensation away.

"I'll need to double the order for towels next weekend," she said, not seeing Sam in the doorway. "In fact, we should probably double the order every weekend until September. I'm booked solid until then."

She seemed to sense his presence then, for she turned around. "Oh, Sam. Good morning." Her gaze didn't quite meet his, and he wondered if she was thinking about the kiss they'd shared the night before. "Sam, this is Ray, who makes my life easier by providing me clean towels and sheets. Every Monday morning he's my favorite man."

The tips of Ray's ears turned pink. "It's a pleasure doing business with you, Daniella," he replied. "I'll see you next week."

As the man left, Daniella closed the door behind him and then turned to Sam. Once again her gaze didn't quite meet his. "You're up early. There's coffee in the pot in here, so help yourself. I haven't started it in the dining room yet."

"I got up early this morning and stepped out on the

porch to watch the sunrise," he replied. "There was something out there for you and Macy. Hang tight and I'll get them."

He left the kitchen and retrieved the flowers and the doll from where he'd placed them moments before, then carried them into the kitchen and set them on the counter.

A tiny frown danced across her forehead as she looked at the pink carnations. "About once a month for the last year we've found little gifts on the front porch. I guess we have a secret admirer."

It was Sam's turn to frown. "What other things have you found?"

"It's almost always flowers for me and some kind of little toy for Macy. The first time it happened was just after I'd had a houseful of guests who had checked out. We found a candy dish and a coloring book and crayons on the front porch. I just assumed it was one of the guests who'd left them as a thank you, but then about a month later there were new presents left." She shrugged. "It's just one of life's little mysteries that I figured would eventually be solved."

"I don't like mysteries," Sam replied flatly.

At that moment the back door opened and Frank came in. "Good morning," he greeted them both. "Gonna be another hot one out there today." He looked from Daniella to Sam. "Uh, did I interrupt something?"

"No, not at all," Daniella replied. "Sam was just getting himself a cup of coffee, and I need to get back to breakfast preparations." She turned toward the oven, and Sam knew any discussion about mysterious gifts or anything else was over.

As far as Sam was concerned the discussion wasn't over; it was merely postponed. He'd been around the place long enough to know that Daniella stayed busy in the mornings but usually had a little downtime in the afternoon.

Both Matt and Frank were in the dining room for breakfast, and the meal passed quickly with the conversation focused on the weatherman's prediction of the possibility of nasty storms for the evening. No one seemed to want to bring up the recent murder.

Sam barely listened to the conversation, distracted by thoughts of his own. Once the meal was over he took his fishing rod and headed for the dock, needing time to process the jumble of thoughts in his head.

The sun was hot, the air oppressive, as he settled into the deck chair and cast his line in the water. He felt as if there was something simmering here, something just under the surface that nobody could see. Call it intuition, gut instinct or whatever, there was no question that Sam was disturbed, and he couldn't quite put his finger on what exactly caused this newest sense of unease.

Certainly kissing Daniella had sent him into a mini tailspin. He wanted her, and that was enough to make him feel uneasy. He also was quite taken with Macy. These were new, alien emotions for him. He'd always been so careful to keep himself from caring about anyone.

There was no question that the appearance of a dead

body in the yard had begun the faint thrum of unease inside him, but the simple fact that Daniella and Macy had been receiving little gifts from an unknown source had that thrum working up to a full throttle.

For you.

That was what Daniella had thought the caller had said to her hours before Samantha Walker had been found murdered. *For you.*

As if her death was a gift, like the flowers and the doll left that morning.

As he reeled in his line and recast it, a knot of tension pressed hard in his chest. He was trained to find the darkness and he felt it nearby, slowly encroaching on the light that shone from Daniella and her daughter.

If somebody was gifting Daniella not only with flowers and candy and the body of a woman who might have been her competition, it spoke of an obsession. What else would someone obsessed be capable of?

"Hi, Mr. Sam." Macy came racing toward him, her blond pigtails bouncing with each step. He couldn't help that the sight of her smiling little face lifted his heart. "Are you catching any fish?"

"Not today, but I'm not trying very hard."

"So what are you doing?" She looped an arm around his shoulder and leaned against his side. Her openness awed him. As a kid he'd always been on guard, afraid to show any feelings at all.

"Just sitting and thinking," he replied.

"I think sometimes, but I don't much like to just sit. Do you have a daddy, Mr. Sam?"

"My daddy is dead." As always thoughts of his father knotted anger inside his chest.

"That's sad." Macy leaned a little closer. "Do you miss him?"

Sam hesitated. "No, not really," he finally replied. "My daddy was kind of a monster."

"And your mommy wasn't a princess?" Macy asked softly.

"No, she wasn't a princess." Realizing it was getting close to lunchtime, Sam began to reel up his line. "But it's okay," he said. "The monster died and I'm here with two princesses and everyone lived happily ever after."

Macy laughed and reached up to kiss him on the cheek. "I love you, Mr. Sam, and I really wish you would be my new daddy."

"Oh, honey, I can't be your new daddy. I'm going to be going home in a couple of days." It felt bad, watching the smile fall from her face, the twinkle in her eyes dim. "But maybe I can come back and visit occasionally and we can hang out together," he added hurriedly.

Who would have thought that the Prince of Darkness could be taken down by a pigtailed little girl with a smile as big as Louisiana?

"That would be nice, but a full-time daddy would be nicer," she replied.

"Macy?" Frank called to her from the yard. "It's time to water that garden of yours."

"I gotta go. I'll see you later." She raced toward Frank and the two of them disappeared around the side of the house.

It was after lunch when Sam found Daniella alone in the kitchen cutting up vegetables for whatever she had planned for dinner.

"Can I talk to you for a minute?" he asked.

She gazed at him warily and set down the knife she'd been using. "If this is about what happened last night, the only thing I have to say is that I normally don't go around kissing my guests. I just made an exception for you."

God, he wanted to kiss her again at that moment, with her cheeks flaming bright and her chin lifted in a show of defiance. Instead he smiled in an attempt to alleviate her defensiveness. "I'm glad you made an exception for me, but that wasn't what I wanted to talk to you about."

"Oh, then what's up?" She directed her gaze to the peeled potatoes on the cutting board in front of her. She picked up her knife and began to dice one of the potatoes.

"Actually I wanted to find out more about these gifts you've been receiving. You said they started coming about a year ago?" She nodded. "And how often do you get them?"

A frown cut across her forehead. "I don't know, about every four to six weeks or so. Why?"

"You aren't curious to find out who is leaving them?"

She stopped cutting and paused with the knife in the air. "Of course I'm curious, but I don't know how to find out who's leaving them. After the second time something was left for us, I asked Frank and Matt and Jeff if any of them were responsible, but they all insisted they weren't, so I just figured eventually whoever it was would make himself known."

"What do you think really happened to Johnny?"

Her eyes flared wide as she stared at him. She placed the knife on the counter and released a deep sigh. "After all this time there are really only two scenarios that make sense. Either he's dead or he chose to disappear. There are times when I believe only death would have kept him away from me and Macy, and there are other times when I wonder if maybe I missed something in the days or weeks leading up to his disappearance. Maybe I didn't realize how overwhelmed he was with a new baby and a business. What difference does it make? Gone is gone and he's nothing more than a part of my past."

"I'm just wondering if he really is a part of the past or if maybe he's behind the gifts you and Macy have received."

She shook her head. "Absolutely not. I know Johnny isn't behind the gifts."

"How can you be so sure?" he asked curiously.

She pointed to the pot of carnations on the table, a faint whisper of revulsion crossing her features. "Carnations were my mother's favorite flowers, and when she died she requested that her casket be covered with them. Johnny knew I absolutely hated carnations after that. He'd never send me something like that." She searched his face with her gaze. "What's this all about, Sam?"

He stared at her for a long moment, wondering if he

should tell her the thoughts that were swirling around in his head or keep them to himself.

He'd come to Bachelor Moon to get away from the darkness of his job, his life, and he'd found a lightness of spirit, good people with Daniella and Macy. And now he was going to bring his darkness to her and he hated it, but he felt as if he didn't have a choice.

"Daniella, it's obvious that somebody close to you has a crush on you, but it's not a good kind of a crush. I think it's a sick obsession, and I believe that along with the flowers and items for Macy, he left you Samantha's body as a gift. I think he's dangerous and you shouldn't trust anyone."

He watched as the light in her eyes doused, replaced by a dark, simmering fear. He hated that the darkness that had always surrounded him had found its way to Bachelor Moon and a woman who was slowly working her way into his heart.

DANIELLA STARED AT HIM, her heart beating an unsteady rhythm. *For you.* The words thundered in her head. Over the last couple of days she'd managed to convince herself that she'd misunderstood what the caller had said to her. But now Sam was forcing her to see the bigger picture, and that picture frightened her.

"What should I do?" she asked.

He frowned. "There isn't much you can do at the moment other than tell the sheriff. What I'm going to do is contact a friend of mine back in Kansas City. Lexie Forbes is a computer geek who can find out anything about anyone. I'm going to have her do some background checks on some of the people here and see what she can dig up. Maybe something will pop that will give us an idea of who is responsible. In the meantime you just need to be careful about what you do and who you're with."

"You've frightened me."

His eyes darkened. "I know, and I'm sorry. Unfortunately this is what I do, Daniella. I see evil everywhere. I suspect people of terrible things."

"What a horrible way to live," she replied softly.

He gave a curt nod to acknowledge her statement and then took a step backward. "I'll let you get back to work. I'm going up to my room to make that call, and I'll see you at dinner."

At that moment the phone in her private quarters rang. She left the kitchen and went into her small living room, where Macy had already answered the phone. "Mommy, it's Lisa. She wants to know if I can spend the night tonight." Macy's eyes sparkled with excitement.

"I need to talk to Tina to make sure it's okay," Daniella replied.

Macy relayed the message to Lisa, then Macy held the phone out to Daniella.

"I think the weather is making Lisa stir-crazy," Tina said. "So I thought it might be nice if she had Macy over for the night. I can pick her up and I'm off tomorrow, so I can bring her back home whenever you need her back."

"It's okay with me if you're sure you want her."

Daniella looked at her daughter, who nodded eagerly. Plus, it seemed like a good idea to get Macy away from all of the madness.

"Actually, you'd be doing me a favor by letting her come. Otherwise Lisa is going to drive me crazy. Why don't I plan on picking her up around four-thirty? I'll order in pizza for dinner and we'll be set for the night."

With the plans made, Daniella returned to the kitchen to finish cutting up the vegetables for the homemade chicken pot pie she'd planned for dinner.

There was no question that her discussion with Sam had disturbed her. Until he'd said it she hadn't tied Samantha's murder to the gifts she and Macy had received over the past year, but his assessment of the situation made a horrifying kind of sense.

Once again she found herself thinking about the men who were close to her. In all the years Frank had worked for her he'd never crossed the line or given her any indication that he might have a crush on her. Frank seemed happiest outside in the sunshine tinkering with the landscaping.

Tina's idea that Matt had a thing for her was ludicrous. Matt might be staying in her bed-and-breakfast for an extended period of time, but he was gone more than he was here. It had been less than a year since he'd lost his wife, and he'd certainly never given her the idea that he might like her as anything more than a friend.

Jeff? Her heart skipped a beat as she thought of the man who had been best man at her wedding, a man who she suspected might have feelings deeper for her than friendship.

It was impossible to think of Jeff as somebody who could kill anyone. He was a criminal defense attorney, a respected and well-liked man in the community.

She thought of all the people she had interaction with, like Ray, who delivered clean sheets and towels, and Billy Sampson, the teenager who occasionally delivered groceries.

It might not even be anyone she did business with, but it could be anyone in the small town who had somehow focused their attention on her, a sick attention that spoke of a dangerous obsession.

"I got my suitcase packed," Macy said, as she came into the kitchen.

"Toothbrush? Clean undies?"

"Oops, I forgot those, but I got all my Barbie dolls packed with their clothes. We're going to play wedding day, and my doll gets to be the bride."

"How about you go back into your room and add that toothbrush and clean underwear to the bridal party?" Daniella suggested. "And while you're in there, you need to straighten up that bookshelf and make sure your room is clean, otherwise there won't be an overnight."

Macy raced out of the kitchen, and Daniella knew she would be occupied with cleaning her room for a while. It took another hour for Daniella to finish up the chicken pot pie and have it ready for the oven.

Sam hadn't showed himself since he'd gone to his

room to make his phone call. She suspected he might be taking an afternoon siesta.

An afternoon nap sounded wonderful to her. She was more tired than usual, and she knew it was from the stress of the events of the last week.

And in less than a week Sam would be gone. He'd be back in Kansas City living his life, doing his job, and she would be left here alone to deal with the mess.

She couldn't help but think that Jim Thompson had stayed away from her the last couple of days because he didn't want any confrontation with Sam. She knew it wasn't fair for her to want Sam to stay, for her to depend on him in any way. And the truth was she didn't only wish he could stay longer because of the bad things that were happening, but also for the good things—like that kiss.

If he stayed longer, if they had more time together, was it possible that that kiss might develop into something deeper, something lasting? Or was he simply a man looking for a quick and easy vacation thrill, and she was his woman of the moment?

She slid the chicken pot pie into the oven and cursed herself for being a fool. Sam had already told her in more ways than one that he was a man who traveled alone, that he had no interest in marriage or children.

"Hey, Daniella," Matt said, as he came into the kitchen.

"Matt! I didn't know you were here."

"Just got here this minute. I was wondering if you've

got anything cold to drink. It's a bear out there. I feel like I've been in a sauna just walking from the car."

"The weatherman is still predicting storms for the evening," she replied, as she opened the refrigerator. "Lemonade?"

"Perfect." He sat at the table as she poured the cold drink for him. "Thanks."

"How is the house coming?" she asked, putting the container back in the refrigerator.

"Coming together great. In fact, we're ahead of schedule. Why? Are you eager to get rid of me?"

"You know better than that. I hardly know you're here most of the time. You know, Tina's stopping by later to pick up Macy for an overnight."

Matt raised one of his eyebrows and looked at her. "Is that a not-so-subtle attempt at matchmaking?"

Daniella shrugged. "You and Tina had a good thing years ago."

"I'm not ready for any kind of a relationship right now. It hasn't even been a year since I lost Cindy."

Daniella wanted to kick herself. It had only been earlier in the day that she'd thought that Matt was still grieving for the wife he'd lost.

"Oh, Matt, I'm sorry. That was thoughtless of me."

He smiled. "Don't worry about it." He downed the lemonade in several long, deep gulps. "I think I'm going to go upstairs and take a nap. It isn't often I have spare time in the afternoon. I'll see you at dinner."

As he left the kitchen, Daniella put his glass in the dishwasher, her thoughts tumbling around in her head.

How could she possibly suspect Matt of having some kind of sick, crazy crush on her? He was still in mourning for his dead wife.

At just after four o'clock she left the house and headed for the bait shack. Every Monday she checked inside to make sure the last round of guests hadn't depleted the bait for the next round of guests. If she found they were running low on anything, then she made out a list for Frank and he took care of the restocking.

A false dusk had fallen, provided by the gathering storm clouds slowly creeping across the sky. The air was like a blanket around her, sticky and without a hint of a breeze.

Daniella had never liked storms. Even though logically she knew thunder and lightning couldn't harm her while she was inside her house, they still frightened her.

She was almost sorry she'd agreed to let Macy spend the night with Tina and Lisa. Although Macy wasn't afraid of bad weather, stormy nights she and Macy usually cuddled together in her bed.

Maybe it will blow right past, she thought as she entered the semidarkness of the bait shack. Frank had apparently already cleaned the place, for the concrete floor was pristine and the dressing table was clean, as well.

It took her only minutes to check the bait in the water wells and the cages, then she went to the small refrigerator to check on the worm supply.

She'd just opened the door when she sensed somebody

behind her. In an instant she was grabbed from behind, and a sickeningly sweet smelling cloth was pressed tightly against her nose and mouth.

Knowing she was in trouble, she tried to scream. She kicked and bucked in an attempt to get free but the arm that held her was like a band of steel.

She tried to hold her breath, but it was impossible, and as she breathed in a wave of dizziness overwhelmed her. Darkness encroached into her brain, and her last conscious thought was that the storm had arrived and she was terrified.

Chapter Six

Sam had gotten in touch with Lexie Forbes hours ago and then had stretched out on his bed for a nap. He didn't expect to hear from Lexie today. She was doing him a favor and would have to work that research in after her regular work had been done.

It was strange. He'd thought talking to Lexie would give him the fever to pack up and get back to Kansas City, back to the job that had taken so much out of him, that had always been his life. But that hadn't happened.

At the moment he felt disconnected from the work that had consumed him and instead felt immersed in Bachelor Moon and Daniella and her daughter. He felt no desire to hurry back to the apartment that had been nothing more than a place to sleep and change clothes.

It was the scream that awakened him, a piercing scream that jolted him not only out of sleep but out of bed.

Macy!

The childish scream came again as he vaulted down

the stairs. It had come from outside. He flew out the front door and saw her in front of the bait shack.

She was on her back on the ground and as he raced toward her he wondered if she'd fallen. And where was Daniella? Surely she should have heard Macy's ear-piercing scream.

"A monster…it was a monster," Macy sobbed, as he reached her side.

"What happened?" Sam asked, as he helped her to a sitting position.

"He shoved me down. The monster shoved me hard and then he ran away." Tears still streaked down her little face, and the roar of an alien emotion—the need to protect—ripped through Sam.

He crouched down next to her. She threw herself into his arms, her little body trembling with fear. "It's okay, Macy, you're safe now," he said. "Can you tell me exactly what happened?"

"I was looking for my mommy and I came out here. I started to go in there." She pointed to the bait shack. "But there was a monster inside. He heard me and he knocked me down and ran away."

Sam's blood ran cold as he processed Macy's words. At that moment Frank came running toward them, a pair of clipping shears in his hand. "What's going on? I was on the other side of the pond and heard Macy scream." He panted to catch his breath.

Sam stood and pulled Macy to her feet. "Why don't you go with Frank into the house and get a drink?"

"I don't want a drink," Macy protested.

Sam exchanged a look with Frank. "Come on, darlin'," Frank said. "I need something cold and you need to come with me." He dropped his shears and grabbed Macy's hand and together they headed toward the house.

Adrenaline pumped through Sam as he looked at the bait shack. What in the hell had happened here? Who was the monster and what had he been doing inside the shack?

As he stepped to the doorway, his heart crashed to his feet and adrenaline spiked through him with a sickening intensity. Daniella was on the floor, her hands behind her back with a length of rope half-tied.

"Daniella!" He fell to the floor at her side and released a gasp of relief as he saw that she was breathing. Quickly he threw the rope to the side and turned her over on her back as her eyelids began to flutter. She moaned, and as consciousness came, she began to fight him.

"Daniella, honey, you're okay. It's Sam. I've got you, you're safe."

As his words penetrated her near hysteria, she relaxed and began to weep. He held her tight, his blood boiling as his mind tried to make sense of things.

It was bad enough that somebody had attacked her, but what iced his heart was that rope around her wrists, the rope that now lay next to her on the concrete floor.

Who had done this and what had been their intention? The rope indicated it wasn't just a simple assault of some kind, but that the perp had other plans besides just attacking her.

"Can you tell me what happened?" he asked when she finally sat up on her own.

She grabbed the back of her head with one hand and winced. "I came in to check on the bait, to see what we might need." Her hand moved from the back of her head to her stomach. "I feel so sick."

"Let's get you out of here and inside." He stood and got her to her feet. She was unsteady, and he held tight to her as they slowly made their way into the kitchen, where Frank and Macy sat at the table.

"Mommy!" Macy jumped out of her chair and ran to Daniella, tears choking out of her. "I was so afraid. I thought the monster killed you."

Daniella collapsed into a chair and hugged Macy tight. "I'm okay."

"What happened?" Frank asked.

"I'd just opened the refrigerator door when somebody grabbed me from behind and pressed a cloth over my nose and mouth." Her voice was thin, shaky, and Sam wanted to slam his fist into the perp's face. "I tried not to breathe." She looked from Sam to Frank and then back again. "I really tried not to breathe but I had to, and when I did I guess I blacked out. I never saw who it was."

"It was monster poison," Macy said softly, her eyes wide with terror.

"No, honey, it wasn't monster poison," Daniella said, some of the strength coming back to her voice. "It was just a bad man."

"Did you see the bad man, Macy? Can you tell me what he looked like?" Sam asked.

"Big and scary," she replied.

"What was he wearing?" Sam knew he couldn't push the little girl too hard, but she was the only hope for some sort of a description.

Macy frowned. "I don't know...I don't remember."

"Did he have hair? What color was his hair?" Frank asked.

Once again tears brimmed in Macy's eyes. "I don't know. He pushed me down and it happened too fast and I don't know what he looked like. He just looked like a monster."

"It's okay," Sam replied, disappointed by her response, but moved by her tears of obvious distress. He crouched down next to her and pulled her into his arms. She came willingly and leaned into him and once again a rage filled Sam.

"Listen to me, Macy. Catching monsters is my job. That's what I do for work. You don't have to worry. I'm going to catch the monster, okay?" Somewhere in the back of his mind he knew he was making a promise he wasn't sure he could keep, but at the moment he meant what he said.

"Really?" she said, her tears disappearing.

"Really," he replied firmly.

A knock on the door halted any further conversation. "That's Tina," Daniella said. "Frank, would you mind letting her in?"

"Can I still spend the night with Lisa?" Macy asked.

Daniella gazed at her daughter. "Of course you can," she replied, knowing that her daughter's instinct was to get away from the danger at home.

"And you'll be okay when I'm gone?"

"I'll be just fine," Daniella assured her. "Sam and Frank are here with me. Go on and get your suitcase."

Tina walked into the kitchen along with a little girl about Daniella's age, with Frank following behind. Macy and her friend disappeared in the direction of Macy's bedroom as Tina gave Daniella a look of concern. "Frank told me what happened. Are you all right?" she asked.

"I'm okay. I just have a touch of a headache." Her words were punctuated by a loud rumble of thunder.

"I need to get some tools inside before it rains," Frank said. "Is there anything else I can do for you, Daniella?"

"No thanks, Frank. Just take care of whatever you need to do, and then you can take off for the night."

Frank left, and soon after Tina and the two girls had gone, as well, leaving Sam alone with Daniella in the kitchen. "We need to call the sheriff," Sam said, as he sat in the chair next to hers.

She frowned. "Is that really necessary? I don't want to deal with Jim Thompson right now."

"I know, but you're going to have to. He needs to know what happened here."

"I'm not sure I know what happened," she replied.

"It's too bad Macy couldn't tell us more about who she saw, but thank God she wasn't hurt."

"She was traumatized. It's possible he knocked her down so fast she didn't get a chance to really process what was happening or who it was." As he thought of Macy's tears, her terror, he once again fought against an anger he'd never allowed himself to feel before.

He got up and grabbed the cordless phone from the counter and then returned to his chair and held it out to her. "Call the sheriff."

She made the call, and when she was finished she leaned back against her chair and gazed at him, her eyes turbulent. "I don't know what to do," she finally said.

"There's nothing to be done until Jim gets here," he replied.

She gave a small shake of her head. "I'm talking about this place, my business."

"What do you mean?"

Another rumble of thunder resounded, and Daniella jumped and wrapped her arms around herself. Sam needed to hold her. He wanted to ease the shadows in her eyes, fix the bright world that had suddenly dimmed for her. Instead he got out of his chair and leaned against the cabinet nearest to where she sat.

"How can I have guests here when they might be in danger? And if I have to cancel all the reservations I have and refund deposits, I'll be in financial ruin." Her voice cracked but she drew in a deep breath and sat up straighter in the chair.

So far, despite what had happened to her, she'd

managed to keep it together, and Sam admired that in her, but she was showing cracks in her facade. The fact that she'd just been attacked and was worried about financial ruin showed him she wasn't quite in touch with the reality of what had happened.

"Daniella, there's no reason to believe that any of your guests would be at risk here. There's no reason to do something impulsive because of what happened. Besides, you have to remember the murder didn't actually happen here on the grounds. It's possible anyone visiting won't even know about what happened."

She gave him a quick, grateful smile that lasted only a minute and then fled. "If this is the same person who has been leaving gifts for me, the same person who you think has a sick crush on me, then why would he try to kill me?"

"I don't think his intention was to kill you."

She gazed at him in confusion. "Then what was his intention?"

Sam drew a deep breath and realized the kitchen had grown dark with the approach of the storm. "He didn't want to kill you," he finally said. "I think what he wanted to do was take you."

"Take me?" The tremor was back in her voice.

Sam nodded. "The gifts he's been leaving you, that was his courtship. Now I'm afraid that the courtship is over and he's ready to close the deal." Lightning flashed in the kitchen, followed by a clap of thunder that sounded like danger closing in.

DANIELLA STAYED STRONG when Jim arrived and interviewed her. He then questioned Sam and Matt, who had napped through the whole incident. Jim went out into the bait shack and looked around but found nothing useful to the investigation. The rope was a clothesline type that was sold in nearly every hardware and discount store in the area.

When he finally left, Daniella felt no closer to safety than she'd felt when he arrived. The thought of somebody wanting to kidnap her and take her off somewhere was horrifying.

She closed the front door and locked it, knowing that Matt was back up in his room and expecting nobody else for the night. Who was doing this to her? She hadn't seen anyone unusual around the place, didn't know who to suspect.

As she left the front door and headed back to the kitchen where Sam was, she realized the entire house smelled of the pot pie she'd put in the oven hours before.

"Oh, my God," she exclaimed. She raced into the kitchen, grabbed two hot mitts and opened the oven door. A faint trail of dark smoke drifted out as she grabbed the large baking dish and pulled it out.

She stared at the blackened crust and then looked at Sam, and to her horror she burst into tears. Logically she knew she wasn't crying about a stupid, burned pot pie, but that didn't halt the cascade of tears that erupted.

Leaning weakly against the counter, embarrassed by

her lack of control, she hid her face in her hands as sobs racked through her.

"Hey," Sam said softly. "Daniella, don't cry. We'll order in pizza for dinner or make sandwiches. Dinner isn't a big deal. Please stop crying."

She shook her head, unable to comply with his wishes. It was as if she'd managed to stuff the horror deep inside her for the last several hours, but it refused to be stuffed any longer.

What on earth had happened to her life in the last week? A week ago her biggest concern had been how to get Macy to brush her teeth before going to bed and what new breakfast casserole she could make for her guests.

Now somebody had killed a woman and attacked her, and until the man was caught she knew she wasn't safe. Her home was no longer a safe haven.

Before she could manage to get control, Sam stepped in front of her and pulled her into his arms. She leaned into him, welcoming the strength of his arms around her, the warmth of his body that after a moment eased some of the chill inside her.

She felt safe with his arms around her and his scent filling her head. It wasn't because it was an FBI agent who held her but because it was Sam.

He was the only one she trusted. And in a week he'd be gone and she'd be here alone to face a madman.

She looked up at him searchingly. "Why is this happening? What did I do?"

His blue eyes darkened and he tightened his arms

around her. "Don't fall into the victim way of thinking. I've seen rape victims who blame themselves for wearing certain clothes, robbery victims who blame themselves for the hour they decided to go shopping, the store they chose to shop at. This isn't your fault and you didn't do anything wrong."

He dropped his arms from around her and took a step backward. "This isn't about you so much as it's about the person who wants you. Something apparently isn't firing right in his head, or he's so maladjusted he believes the only way to have you is to take you against your will. We can't know exactly what's going on with him until we've caught him, but I doubt if there is anything different you could have done to stop this."

Daniella moved to the counter that held the burned chicken pot pie and placed the dish in the sink. "So how do we catch him?" she asked, as she began to scrap the pie down the garbage disposal.

"I'm hoping he'll make a mistake. This attack on you is a definite escalation of whatever drives him. Something set him off, a trigger of sorts. It was damned ballsy of him to attempt to grab you right here on the property, and in the middle of the afternoon with so many other people around."

He sat in a chair at the table and Daniella was aware of his gaze on her while she finished scraping out the last of the pot pie. She then placed the baking dish in the dishwasher and turned to face him.

"So what happens now?"

"We make sandwiches?" He offered her a smile that further eased the tension inside her.

By the time they had eaten and she had taken up a platter of sandwich and chips to Matt, the rain finally arrived, pelting the windows with ferocity as thunder and lightning returned.

At eight Macy called to check in, and the sound of her happy voice was like a balm to Daniella's jagged nerves.

After the call Daniella and Sam moved into the common room, where they sat on the sofa to continue discussing the events that had occurred.

"Jim said he's going to check to see if anyone in town has access to chloroform. From what you described that sounds like what he used to press against your face," Sam said.

"I just don't have much faith in Jim and his team coming up with anything concrete," she confessed.

"When he left here he was going to Frank's cabin to talk to him about what happened. Jim seems to be taking the whole thing seriously. No matter what happened between the two of you in the past, you need to give him a chance now."

Daniella wondered if he was just saying that because in a week he'd be gone and she'd be left depending only on Jim Thompson to find the man who killed Samantha, the man who attacked her.

"I know you have a life to return to, but I wish you didn't have to leave." She looked down at her hands in her lap, not wanting him to see her need for him in her eyes.

He reached out and took one of her hands in his, and she looked up to see his eyes dark and unfathomable. "At least you know now that there's danger near. You know you have to be careful. Don't go anywhere that's isolated, be aware of your surroundings. If you leave the house for anything make sure somebody is with you. If you're smart you'll be fine."

He dropped her hand and reached out to tuck a strand of her hair behind her ear. "A lot of things can happen in a week. Maybe by the time I pack my bags to go home Jim will have made an arrest, and you won't have to worry anymore."

She told herself that he owed her nothing, that he had a life to return to, a life that didn't include any desire for a wife, a family. Besides, he was just a guest here, a guest who had gone above and beyond for her in a time of crisis. She had no business wanting him to stay, no business wanting him at all.

But she did want him. Even now, just sitting next to him, despite everything that had happened to her, a small sizzle of desire for him burned inside her.

"You should call it a night," he finally said. He stood and held out a hand to her to help her up.

She took his hand and stood so close to him that her desire shot higher. Did she want him because she was still afraid? Because that fear had created a need to be held, to not be alone while the rain fell and somewhere out there a crazy man plotted evil?

Maybe, but her desire for him was also tied to the fact that sometimes, when he looked at her, she felt half breathless, and that the scent of him made her want to crawl into his arms and never leave. She had wanted him before Samantha's body had appeared in her yard, before she had known that any danger existed.

"Daniella? Are you all right?" he asked.

She realized she held his hand too tight and had been staring at him as her brain raced with her thoughts. "No, I'm not all right. I don't want to be alone, Sam. Would you come to my room and sit with me for a little while longer?"

Once again it was impossible to read his eyes. He hesitated a moment and then nodded. "I can do that."

She left a small lamp on in the common room and then, after she checked to make sure all the doors were locked, they went through the kitchen and into her private quarters.

Her bedroom was just large enough to hold a double bed and a dresser. She'd given Macy the larger of the two bedrooms in this area of the house, knowing her daughter would need room to play.

As they entered the bedroom Sam stood just inside the door, obviously ill at ease. She went to her dresser and pulled out her nightgown, a simple, white cotton shift. "I'll just get ready for bed and be right back." She disappeared into the bathroom and wondered if he'd still be there when she came out.

As she changed her clothes and brushed her teeth she consciously kept her thoughts away from what had happened in the bait shack, willed herself to think only about Sam and what she wanted to happen now.

It had been years since she'd thought of making love to a man, years since she'd entertained any desire for anyone. Sam had stirred something in her that she'd almost forgotten she could feel: he'd made her remember she was a young woman who had always enjoyed sex, who wanted to experience it again with him.

There was no illusion of a happily-ever-after here. He was a temporary man who would be gone in a week, and at the moment that felt okay. Maybe he was just what she needed to ease back into a life open to romance, a way to close her old life and grasp a new one that might include the possibility of romance.

She'd always done everything safe in her life. She'd married her childhood sweetheart; she'd tried to be the perfect wife and mother. Since Johnny's disappearance she'd made all her decisions based on hard facts and what was in the best interest of Macy and the business.

But at this moment she felt like doing something risky, something just for herself. She wanted to have sex with Sam Connelly. For one night she didn't want to feel like an overworked business owner; she didn't want to feel like a mother; she wanted to feel hot and desirable and all woman, and she knew Sam was just the man to make her feel that way.

When she left the bathroom she half-expected Sam to be gone, but he stood just inside her bedroom like a sentry on duty. She stopped in front of him, her heart beating rapidly.

She knew she should feel self-conscious standing before him in nothing but the cotton shift and panties, but as his eyes narrowed and she sensed a new tension roiling off him, she felt nothing but desire for him.

"I made an exception the other night to kiss you, and now I want to make another exception for you," she said. She reached up and placed a hand in the center of his chest, his skin radiating warmth through the fabric of his T-shirt.

"What kind of an exception?" His voice sounded deeper than usual.

For a single wild moment she wondered if she'd misread him, if perhaps she'd mistaken the desire she saw shining in his eyes sometimes when he looked at her, if she'd misread the signals she'd thought he was giving off.

She ignored the sudden trembling inside her, a symptom of uncertainty, a fear of rejection. "I never sleep with my guests, but I'd make an exception tonight with you."

She knew she'd shocked him by the flare of his eyes and the fact that he took a step backward from her. "Daniella, you've had a rough day. I don't want you making a decision now that you'll regret later."

"You're right, I've had a rough day, but I'm thinking as clearly as I've ever thought in my life. I want you, Sam. I know better than to wish for a lifetime with you. I know you're only going to be here another week and you have a life of your own. I just want tonight in your arms."

He took a step closer to her and reached out and touched a strand of her hair and then cupped her cheek. "No expectations? No regrets?"

"None," she replied.

"In that case, I thought you'd never ask." As he took her into his arms and kissed her with an intensity that stole her breath away, Daniella recognized that he was probably going to break her heart if the person who was after her didn't succeed in their sick plan first.

Chapter Seven

Sam didn't want to think about mistakes. He knew he was probably making one, but he didn't want to think about anything other than having Daniella naked and panting in his arms.

He needed to believe her words of assurance about knowing the score, because he wanted her more than he'd wanted any woman in a very long time.

When the kiss ended she moved to one side of the bed and pulled back the blue-flowered spread, then slid beneath the sheets. She looked beautiful in the soft glow from the lamp on the nightstand.

A vacation hookup, that was all he was looking for, and she said that she understood that. He wanted desperately to believe her. He walked to the other side of the bed and pulled his wallet from his jeans. He had a couple of condoms inside. For him safe sex had always been the only option.

He placed the wallet on the nightstand and then pulled his shirt over his head, aware of her watching him. He sat on the edge of the bed and kicked off his shoes, then took off his socks. Standing once again, his hands went to his button fly as he held her gaze with his. "At any time if you change your mind all you have to do is tell me. Everything stops if you want it to, and no hard feelings."

She laughed, and he wanted to capture the sound of it to take back to Kansas City with him, a memory he could enjoy when the darkness got too intense. "I'm not going to change my mind, Sam. I want you."

"And you have no idea how much I want you," he replied. Her declaration lit a fire in him that had him out of his jeans in seconds. Clad only in his briefs, he joined her in the bed as she reached out and turned off the bedside lamp. The room was plunged into a darkness broken only by the intermittent flashes of lightning outside the window.

He gathered her into his arms and easily found her lips for another kiss that quickly had him at full arousal. It would be easy to take what he needed, fast and furious, but that was not what he wanted.

Aware that it had been a long time since she'd been with anyone, he wanted to give her a night to remember. He wanted to take his time and give her as much pleasure as possible.

Her hands smoothed down his back as the kiss continued, exploring and sensually stroking. Her body was hot beneath the cotton nightgown, and her sweet scent filled his head.

His mouth left her lips and traveled down the length of her neck, nipping and tasting her as her fingers dug slightly into his back.

He slid his hands from around her to caress the front of her, lingering over her breasts where the cool cotton warmed quickly and he could feel her erect nipples through the thin fabric.

She gasped slightly at the intimate touch but encouraged him by softly murmuring his name. Rain continued to pelt the windows along with an occasional burst of lightning and the low rumble of thunder.

Sam took it slow, kissing her deeply, stroking the length of her and fighting his own desire for instant fulfillment. It was she rather than he who grew impatient with the barrier of clothing between them.

She pulled away from him and sat up. In one smooth, graceful movement she swept her nightgown over her head. At that moment a flash of lightning gave him a visual, and his breath caught in his chest at her beauty.

She removed her panties, as well, and as she moved back into his arms, her bare breasts against his chest only managed to further enflame him. "You are so beautiful," he murmured, as he nuzzled her neck.

"You make me feel beautiful," she replied breathlessly. "But I'm naked and you aren't, and I want you naked, Sam."

God, he loved a woman who knew her mind and wasn't afraid to ask for what she wanted. He kicked off his briefs, and this time when they came together it was all hot bare skin and breathless sighs.

He slid down her body to capture a tip of her breast in his mouth. As he teased the turgid nipple with his tongue, she tangled her fingers into his hair and moaned with pleasure.

Caressing slowly down her stomach with his other hand, he felt her tension as he finally found the core of her heat. She gasped again at the intimate touch and arched up to meet him.

Her excitement fed his own, and it was all he could do to control the urge to crawl between her thighs and take her in several deep, long thrusts.

Not yet, he told himself. He didn't want to give in to his own need yet. Instead he focused on her, on moving his fingers to find the specific spot that would bring her the most pleasure.

It took only moments for her to respond to him. She whispered his name once again, her voice filled with tension as he increased the speed, the pressure, of his touch.

"Oh," she moaned, as her entire body stiffened. "Oh, yes." A deep tremor overtook her as she moaned deep and low in her throat. Suddenly she went limp and gasped with a laugh of sheer delight. "That was amazing."

"We're not finished yet," he replied, and took her mouth with his.

As they kissed she reached down and grabbed him, her fingers circling his hardness. Her touch electrified him, and when she moved her fingers up and down, stroking his shaft with sweet intent, he knew he couldn't stand it a minute longer, that he had to have her now.

He rolled away from her and grabbed his wallet from

the nightstand. His fingers shook as he pulled out one of the condoms and quickly ripped the package open. It took him only a moment to have the condom in place and then he turned back to her.

She was ready, and she opened her legs to welcome him. He moved over her and slowly entered her. She sighed his name as he closed his eyes against the wild sensation of her tight heat.

Nuzzling her neck, he began to move his hips against hers. Her hands grasped his shoulders as he stroked in and out, lost in the pleasure, lost in her.

As his movements increased in rhythm he found her mouth once again and the kiss was wild, frantic with need and something else—an emotion he didn't want to analyze.

When his climax came it washed over him like thundering waves, crashing through his entire body.

When it was over he collapsed to the side of her, his breaths beginning to slow with each minute that passed.

"I'll make an exception for you any day of the week, Mr. Sam," Daniella said.

He released an uncharacteristic laugh. "That was fairly amazing."

"You rocked my world. You made my toes curl," she replied.

"Glad to be of service." He slid out of the bed and headed toward the bathroom.

"Sam?"

He paused in the doorway and looked back in her direction.

"You are coming back, aren't you?" There was no levity in her voice.

Normally this was the time to cut and run. No time to cuddle or murmur meaningless sweet talk. No sense hanging around once the deed was done. But once again that alien emotion that he didn't want to examine rushed through him. "Yeah, I'm coming back," he finally replied.

When he returned to the room he slid back into the bed and she came immediately into his arms. She laid her head against his chest and released a sigh of obvious contentment.

"Tell me about Kansas City. I've never been there before," she said.

"It's a nice city. Big enough to have everything anyone would need yet with a small-town feel."

"Did you grow up there?"

"Born and raised there." He stroked a hand down her silky back as she snuggled closer against him.

"Do you own a house there?"

"Nah, I rent an apartment. It's nothing fancy, furnished minimally. I'm not there enough to have it feel like home." He frowned. He hadn't thought about it before, but he hadn't felt like he'd had a home since he'd been a kid, and even then his home had grown increasingly fraught with the whisper of danger.

"You've made a nice place here for Macy to grow up," he said.

"Thanks. It's a delicate balance, seeing to the needs of all the guests and making sure Macy doesn't suffer from it. Thankfully she is outgoing and enjoys meeting new people. She has definitely taken a shine to you." Daniella's words were coming slower and her voice was filled with drowsiness.

"I haven't spent much time around kids, but she seems pretty special."

"Hmm, special," she murmured in response.

Within minutes he knew that she was sound asleep. Her breathing had the long, steady rhythm of the exhausted. He realized the storm had passed. Rain no longer beat against the windows, and there was an absence of thunder.

The scent of Daniella filled his head, that sweet fragrance of a floral perfume coupled with sleeping woman. She could be the exception to his rule. If he decided he wanted a relationship with a woman, Daniella would be the woman he would choose.

But he wasn't breaking his rules. Just because he'd slept with her and it had been amazing didn't mean he was the right man for her. He wasn't the right man for any woman.

He slid out of bed and padded naked to the window, where he peered out into the night. A sliver of the moon was visible through the thinning clouds, and even through the window he could hear the deep croak of happy bullfrogs from the lake.

Contentment filled him, a strange contentment that he'd never felt before. He thought about the past week that he'd spent here, and he realized he'd found happiness in a jar of fireflies and a little girl's laughter. He'd found joy in Daniella's warm smile and the light that shone from her pretty eyes.

If he allowed himself, he could be happy in a place like this, with a woman like her. If he permitted himself, he could see himself opening his heart to accept whatever was offered to him here.

But he wouldn't allow it. He refused to permit it. The best thing he could do for Macy and Daniella was walk away from them. They deserved the best and that wasn't him.

He turned away from the window and crept back to the bed, where he got in next to the sleeping Daniella. She turned toward him and placed a hand on his chest, still sleeping peacefully. The gesture spoke of trust, of an easy intimacy that brought a knot to his chest.

Somebody wanted her. Somebody wanted Daniella enough to attempt a kidnapping. And if Sam was right that person had already committed murder.

He was torn between his need to escape Daniella and Macy before they got too deeply into his heart and the desire to protect Daniella against the danger he felt growing closer with each minute that passed.

Hopefully Lexie would call the next day with some background information on some of the players, and hopefully that information would make clear who presented the danger to Daniella.

He released a small sigh. She'd reeled him in. There

was no way he could walk away from here in a week if nothing had been resolved.

He had to see this through. This was what he did— catch monsters. And there was a monster out there with his eye on Daniella. Sam would stay until that monster was caught and then, no matter how difficult it was, he'd walk away from here. Because that was what he did best of all: he walked away.

DANIELLA AWOKE SUDDENLY, unsure what had pulled her from her sleep. It took her only a minute to realize it was Sam. He was obviously in the throes of a bad dream.

"No," he muttered as his legs thrashed wildly beneath the sheets. "No…stop!" His voice grew louder. In the dawn light she saw his features twist in an expression of horror.

"Sam," she said gently, and laid a hand on his tense shoulder. "Sam, wake up."

He bolted upright, eyes wide open in alarm. He stared at her as if she were a specter from his nightmare landscape. His chest rose and fell with each quickened breath.

Recognition filled his eyes and he swiped a hand down his face. "What time is it?"

"Almost six. You were having a nightmare."

"Yeah, sorry." Tension still rode his shoulders, and his eyes remained slightly haunted.

"You remember what you were dreaming about?" She wanted to stroke her fingers across his forehead, curl up next to him and hold him until the dark haunting left his eyes and the tension eased from his body.

"Yeah, I remember. It wasn't so much a nightmare as a memory." Some of the tension left his shoulders as he once again rubbed a hand across his jaw.

"A memory about what?" She placed her hand on his forearm and slid closer to him.

He hesitated a long moment. "About the day my father shot my mother dead and then tried to shoot me." His words were flat as he held her gaze.

Shock rivuleted through her, a shock she tried not to show. "How old were you when this happened?"

"Fifteen." He finally broke eye contact with her and stared to the opposite wall of the room. He appeared lost in his thoughts, and she could tell by the look on his face that those thoughts weren't pleasant.

"Was your father mentally ill?"

A rough bark of laughter erupted from him as he looked at her once again. "No, he was just a brutal bastard."

She squeezed his arm. "Tell me about that day." Maybe if he talked about it he wouldn't have his nightmares, she thought. Maybe it was something he needed to talk about.

"There isn't a lot to tell. I got home from school and found my dad in the kitchen with my mother. He had a shotgun pointed to her head and told me he was going to kill her and then kill me."

"Had he done something like this before?"

"Nothing that extreme, but he could be a violent man,

especially when he drank, and he drank a lot. Usually he just raged, slammed things around and cussed. That day was different. He seemed unnaturally calm and focused. He told me what he was going to do and then he did it. He shot my mother in the head, and as the shotgun turned in my direction I dove into the living room and then ran out the front door."

His muscles beneath her fingers grew taut once again as he continued. "I heard the blast of the shotgun as I ran, and I finally hid behind a tree in the neighbor's yard. They'd heard the gunshots, too, and called the police. When the police arrived they discovered that my mom was dead and so was my father. He'd apparently killed himself after I ran away."

"Oh, Sam," she said softly, and wrapped her arms around him. He leaned into her as a weary sigh escaped him. She couldn't imagine what kind of scars had been left inside him by the experience, but she wished she could heal them all by her willpower alone.

He pulled away from her and offered her a tight smile. "It's over and done and just a little piece of my past that haunts my nights sometimes."

It was obvious by his tone of voice that he didn't want to talk about it anymore. He kissed her on the forehead and then got out of the bed. "I'd better get out of here and back to my own room before somebody sees us together and we start a small-town scandal."

She smiled. "I've always wondered what it would be like to be a scandalous woman."

"Stick with me, honey, and you'll find out." With these words he left her room.

She stretched, reluctant to get out of the bed that smelled of him. As she thought of what they'd shared before they'd gone to sleep a sweet warmth suffused her.

It had been everything his kiss had promised, hot and sexy, and utterly amazing. Her body still retained the imprint of his. Eventually that would fade, but she knew the imprint he was leaving on her heart would take far more time to forget.

Her feeling of satisfaction didn't last long as she thought of what Sam had just shared with her, and the fact that there was still somebody out there who wanted her, somebody with a sick obsession.

She finally got out of bed and went into the bathroom to shower and get ready for the day. Hopefully it would be a day of no drama, no danger.

An hour later she was just pulling cinnamon rolls out of the oven when Jeff appeared at the back door. "It seems like I'm always hearing about something bad that happened to you after the fact," he said, as she let him into the kitchen. "The attack on you was the talk of the diner last night."

"Nobody mentioned any potential suspects, did they? Because I can't imagine who it was," she explained. She gestured him to the table and grabbed a cup from the cabinet.

As she poured him a cup of coffee and then carried it to the table he looked at her with a narrowed gaze.

"For all you've been through you certainly don't look the worse for wear. In fact, you look happy."

"The storm has passed, the sun is shining and there isn't much I can do about what happened yesterday."

A frown tracked across his forehead. "I wish I would have been here for you. You must have been terrified."

"I was," she admitted. "But Sam was here and he definitely helped make me feel safe."

"He did, huh? When is he going home?"

"This Friday," she replied, and tried not to feel the sadness that threatened to sweep over her at thoughts of him no longer being in the house.

Jeff took a sip of his coffee, then set the cup back on the table. "At least with the attack on you yesterday Jim Thompson has to realize somebody is preying on the women of Bachelor Moon."

"I was grateful he seemed to take the attack on me seriously."

"He'd better," Jeff said indignantly. "That's his job."

"Speaking of jobs, I'd better get these eggs scrambled for breakfast. Are you going to stick around to eat?"

"No thanks." He drained his coffee cup and got up to carry it to the sink. He placed his hands on her shoulders and gazed into her eyes. "Daniella, if you need me to move in here for a while until this person is caught, I can do that. At least you'd have somebody you can trust here with you."

"That's not necessary, but I appreciate the offer. At

least for the next couple of days I have somebody I trust completely with me," she replied.

"When Superhero Sam leaves, the offer still stands," he replied.

Daniella laughed and moved away from him. "I'll definitely keep that in mind."

It was only after Jeff left that dark thoughts entered her mind. It had become increasingly obvious to her that Jeff would like to take their friendship to a deeper level.

Had his desire for her grown into something darker? Had he attacked her yesterday in an effort to kidnap her or in some crazy attempt to force her to turn to him?

She'd just placed breakfast on the table when Tina called to ask if it was okay for Macy to spend the day with her and Lisa and that she'd bring Macy home around supper time. Daniella agreed, with the understanding that she'd reciprocate by having Lisa over after things calmed down at the bed-and-breakfast.

Sam, Frank and Matt were all at breakfast. Each time she entered the dining room warmth swept through her as she saw the man she'd slept with the night before.

"I can't believe I slept through all the excitement last night," Matt said, as Daniella delivered a bowl of fresh fruit to the table. "I was shocked when Jim woke me up to question me."

"Too many hours selling insurance and checking on the builders at your new house," Daniella said.

"You got that right," Matt replied. "I feel like I've been burning the candle at both ends for too long." He smiled at Daniella. "But I'm glad you're okay and that Sam and Frank were there to help you."

"I'm glad, too," she replied.

"Hopefully the whole experience didn't give you nightmares last night," Frank said.

She glanced at Sam, who smiled, a secretive, sexy smile that made every moment of the night before flash through her head. This was one of the things she'd missed, a shared glance filled with heat and intimacy with a man who made her heart sing.

"No," she replied. "I slept like a baby."

After breakfast Frank went outside to begin his day of work, Matt left for his insurance office and Sam disappeared into the common room when his cell phone rang.

As Daniella cleaned up the kitchen she thought of the weekend to come. Sam would be leaving and three couples would be arriving on Saturday. She tried not to focus on the heartache that threatened to take hold of her as she thought of Sam going home.

She'd known all along that he was nothing more than a guest in her place of business. The fact that she'd slept with him certainly made telling him goodbye more difficult, but she had only herself to blame for that.

She was the one who had initiated the lovemaking between them. She was the one who had told him there would be no regrets.

At least she'd be busy for the weekend when he departed and hopefully wouldn't have too much spare time to examine the emotions he stirred in her.

She poured herself a cup of coffee, moved to the back door and stared outside, and her thoughts turned to the man who had once been her husband.

She had loved Johnny with all her heart and soul. In the years of their marriage her love for him had never wavered. She'd believed they would be together forever and when he'd disappeared her entire world had splintered apart.

Sipping her coffee she realized that if nothing else Sam had made her realize she'd truly moved on and put Johnny in her past, and that her heart was open and ready to love again.

"Hey."

She turned to see Sam standing in the doorway of the kitchen. "Hey," she replied, and stepped away from the door.

"You have a few minutes?"

"Sure, what's up?" She motioned him to the table where they both sat.

"I just heard from my lab-rat friend, Lexie. She had some information about some of the people who are close to you." He pulled out a notepad where he'd made notes.

A knot of anxiety formed in Daniella's chest as she waited for what he'd learned. His features were pulled taut, as if the information he'd gathered wasn't good.

"You're making me nervous," she said.

The tight smile he gave her did nothing to alleviate her nervousness. "First of all, I had Lexie check into what she could find out about Johnny."

The tension inside her screamed just a little bit and her throat went dry. "What did she find out? That he's on a Caribbean island and married to a half-naked native girl?"

Sam shook his head. "Nothing. She found absolutely nothing. When he disappeared from Bachelor Moon it's like he fell off the face of the earth. His Social Security number has never been used, and there's no record that he owns property of any kind. There are no vehicles registered to him, and he hasn't filed income tax since the year he disappeared."

"So what does that mean?"

He leaned back in his chair. "It means he's either living carefully, completely under any radar, or he's dead."

She nodded. "So that's nothing new. Those have always been the only two real possibilities."

"I didn't realize Frank wasn't originally from Bachelor Moon," Sam continued.

"I think he'd just moved to town when he took the job with Johnny at the plant," Daniella explained. "If I remember right, he was originally from Chicago."

"The information Lexie pulled up on him didn't send off any alarms. His work history before coming to Bachelor Moon is spotty, mostly menial jobs. He's had one speeding ticket in his lifetime of driving and has never been married."

"What about Jeff?" she asked.

"Pretty much the same thing. Never married, no red flags and appears on paper to be an upstanding citizen.

Matt is a little more interesting. What did he tell you about his wife's death?"

She looked at him in surprise. "He just told me she'd died. I assumed it was some sort of illness. Why?" A new knot of anxiety formed in her chest as she saw that Sam's eyes had gone dark and flat. "Is the official story something different?"

"Cindy Rader was found dead in a dry bathtub. She'd suffered a severe head wound that killed her."

Daniella frowned. "Where was Matt when it happened?"

"According to the reports he was sitting in his living room reading the paper. Eventually he went to look for her and found her dead in the tub."

"So, it was a tragic case of a slip and fall," Daniella said, wishing she'd refilled her coffee cup for the warmth the brew might provide.

"Not so simple," Sam countered, his eyes still far too dark to put her at ease. "At the time of Cindy's death there were rumors of marital problems between the two. They were also having some major financial issues, and there was a million-dollar life insurance policy on Cindy with Matt as the sole beneficiary. The investigating officers believed he'd killed her, that somehow they'd fought and he slammed her head into the tub."

Daniella was stunned and more than a little sickened by what he'd said. "Then why isn't he in jail?"

"No evidence to prove what they believed." He released a sigh and leaned forward. "Of course none of this proves that Matt killed Samantha or that he's the person who is after you."

"But if what the police believed about his wife's death was true, then that means I've had a murderer in my house for the last couple of months." Despite the warmth of the kitchen a cold wind blew through her.

Chapter Eight

Soon, Sam thought as he sat on the porch. A few more days and he'd be out of here, back to his own life, his old job. The last two days had been uneventful.

He'd checked in with Jim Thompson and told him what he'd learned with the background checks Lexie had conducted. Jim had been surprisingly grateful to Sam for sharing what he'd learned.

"I've got to confess I'm no closer to solving Samantha's death than I was when we found her beneath that tree," he'd said. "I was hoping the knife might yield some kind of evidence, but it was just an old, ordinary butcher knife as sharp as a scalpel. There were no prints or anything unusual about it except for how sharp it was."

Jim went on to say that he also had no motives or suspects for the attack on Daniella. Sam had been vigilant in making sure Daniella wasn't alone again except when she went to her room for the night.

Daniella had wondered if perhaps the failed attempt to kidnap her had forced the perp to give up his plan, perhaps move his obsession to somebody else, but Sam feared that the failed attempt had only stoked the hunger of the person responsible, a hunger for Daniella and nobody else.

He sat up straighter in his chair as a car pulled up the driveway. Jeff. He'd stopped by to visit with Daniella for the past two nights. Sam didn't move from his chair as Jeff parked his car and got out, the early evening sunshine sparking on his blond hair.

Sam suspected that Jeff had sensed something going on between him and Daniella and his visits were an attempt to mark his territory where Daniella was concerned.

"Evening," he said to Sam, as he reached the porch.

"Back at you," Sam replied. "Beautiful night."

"It is," Jeff agreed. He nodded at Sam and then disappeared through the front door.

Sam remained seated, although his natural instinct was to get up and go inside, to make sure that Daniella wasn't alone with Jeff. But he trusted that if Jeff was the culprit, he wouldn't try anything after having been seen by Sam. The person they were after was far craftier than that.

Jeff was inside for about thirty minutes, and when he came out he stopped in front of Sam's chair, an edge of belligerence riding the upthrust of his chin.

"I'm not a stupid man. I know there's something going on between you and Daniella," he said. His brown eyes narrowed as Sam stood. "Maybe this is something you do? Big important G-man rides into town and takes advantage of women in danger?"

"I'm not taking advantage of anyone," Sam replied in a calm, even tone. He wasn't about to get in a pissing match with another alpha dog. "Besides, you don't have to worry. I'm leaving here in two days."

"Yeah, well, I think you are taking advantage, and I just want you to know if you hurt Daniella in any way I'll hunt you down and do more than hurt you."

"Nice trash talk for a defense attorney," Sam replied drily.

Jeff's face flushed. "I'm not talking to you as a defense attorney; I'm talking to you as a man. Stay away from her. She's had enough heartache in her life without you adding to it." He didn't wait for Sam's reply but instead stomped off the porch and got into his car.

Sam didn't know whether to be amused or concerned. This was a side of Jeff he hadn't seen before. Intense, seething with suppressed anger, Sam had for a moment recognized a darkness in Jeff.

Jeff's car roared to life and he flew down the driveway. *Interesting,* Sam thought, as he sat back down. Was it possible that Jeff had loved his best friend's bride, that perhaps he'd seen Johnny as an obstacle to get through in order to possess his perfect woman? Had Johnny been killed, or had he simply run from the responsibility of wife and baby and business?

"Mr. Sam." Macy flew out the front door, her eyes sparkling with excitement. "Mommy and I are having an ice cream party and we want you to come."

"Ice cream party? Sounds like something I don't want

to miss," he replied, grateful for the diversion from his own troubling thoughts.

Macy grabbed his hand and pulled him out of his chair. "We have different flavors of ice cream and syrup and marshmallows and sprinkles!"

"Sprinkles? I love sprinkles," Sam replied, and was gifted with one of Macy's delightful giggles.

They entered the kitchen where Daniella was getting out bowls to set on the table, which was already laden with everything needed to make an awesome sundae or a banana split. "Wow, looks serious," he said with a smile to Daniella.

She returned his smile. "We take our ice cream nights very seriously."

"Jeff didn't want to stay for ice cream night?" he asked.

"I didn't invite him to stay." Daniella pointed to the chairs at the table. "Sit and let the fun begin."

As he and Macy sat at the table she pulled out three half-gallon containers of ice cream: one vanilla, one chocolate and one strawberry. She set them on the table and then took the seat between Sam and Macy. "Dig in."

She laughed as all three of them reached for the chocolate at the same time. "Great minds think alike."

There was no way her mind could be thinking like his, for as he saw her laughter shining from her eyes and curving her lips he wanted nothing more than to take her into the bedroom and repeat the experience of making love to her.

Instead he filled his bowl with vanilla ice cream and smothered it in chocolate syrup, hoping that satisfying his sweet tooth would somehow diminish his desire for a woman who would never be a part of his future.

"I'm gonna have syrup and bananas and whipped cream and sprinkles," Macy announced, as she worked on her concoction.

As they created their decadent desserts, they chatted about everything and nothing. Their laughter filled not only the kitchen but also some of the empty places inside Sam's soul.

This was what it was like, he thought. This was what it was like to have a family, to laugh together and act silly and not worry, because you were among people who cared about you.

He had a sudden flash of memories from his early childhood, of occasional movie nights with popcorn and laughter, before his father had started with his raging, before things had gotten bad between his mother and father, before the monster inside his dad had fully formed.

"Mr. Sam, you forgot your sprinkles," Macy said, pulling him from his memories.

"I did, didn't I?" He grabbed the bottle and liberally dosed his ice cream.

A few sprinkles, a little ice cream and the company of a beautiful woman and her daughter could probably cure diseases, he thought. At the moment it was impossible to entertain dark thoughts or ruminate about the past. He was in the moment and loving it, and that shocked him as much as finding Samantha's body beneath the tree in the yard.

By the time they finished their ice cream Daniella sent Macy in to get ready for her bath, and he and Daniella cleared the table. She placed their bowls in the sink, and he grabbed her arm and twirled her around to look at him.

"This was fun," he said, as he pulled her closer against him, unable to squash his desire to hold her.

She smiled, that beautiful gesture that lit her eyes and curved her lush lips. "It was fun. I try to plan something like this every once in a while. You should be at one of our pizza-making parties."

He wished he could be at all their parties, have night after night of laughter with Daniella and Macy. He ran his hands across her slender shoulders. "You know what my nickname is? The Prince of Darkness, that's how all my coworkers refer to me. On the day my father shot my mother I lost all my laughter, any joy I might have found in life. I immersed myself in the darkness of my job and forgot that there was anything good in life."

She reached up and placed her palm against his jaw and he wanted to fall into the softness, the bright light shining in her eyes.

"I just want to thank you, Daniella. You and Macy helped me find my laughter again." He couldn't stand it another minute, he had to kiss her sweet, soft lips.

She tasted of chocolate and heat, of desire and dreams, and as she wound her arms around his neck he wanted all of her. As he pulled her more tightly against him he knew she could feel his arousal. He also knew that nothing would happen between them again, that no matter how badly he wanted to make love to her again he wouldn't go there.

In fact, although she couldn't know it, this was a goodbye kiss. He had to start separating himself from her. He had to begin to gain some distance so his final goodbye in two days' time wouldn't be so painful.

The Prince of Darkness had found his heart and he didn't like it. He knew Daniella was falling for him. He could see it in her eyes, taste it on her lips. And he was falling for her. He hadn't seen it coming. When he'd pulled up here for a two-week vacation the last thing he'd expected to find was a woman who would stir up the desire for things he'd never considered.

He cared enough about Daniella and Macy to walk away from them. He wasn't what they needed in their lives, and they were far better off without him.

Reluctantly he ended the kiss. Daniella looked up at him, a hint of tears in her eyes. "I have to admit it, Sam—I'm going to miss you when you're gone."

He dropped his arms from around her and stepped back. "Once things calm down in your life and Jim has the bad guy behind bars you probably won't even remember me."

"That's not true," she replied. Her lower lip trembled slightly. "I'm going to remember you the rest of my life, Sam Connelly."

At that moment Macy called from the bathroom, and Daniella left the room. Sam drew a deep breath and tried to ignore the fact that he was leaving her here alone and vulnerable.

He told himself he couldn't put his own life on hold forever, that solving this crime had never been his job, his responsibility.

In the best of all possible worlds this would be solved in two days' time and he would leave here knowing that the culprit was behind bars. But the truth of the matter was that it could take weeks, even months, before this case would be resolved.

Despite the fact that night had fallen outside, Sam felt the need to get some air, to step into the hot humid night and breathe something other than the sweet scent of Daniella.

The minute he stepped outside he spied them—a box of candy and a coloring book. His stomach clenched as he saw that a small note card was taped to the top of the box of candy.

He went back into the kitchen and opened the cabinet under the sink where he knew Daniella kept rubber gloves. He pulled them on and then returned to the porch.

He seriously doubted that any fingerprints had been left on the items, but on the off chance that the perp had gotten careless, Sam didn't want to screw up what might be important evidence.

He carried the items back into the house and set them on the kitchen table, then removed the gloves and went to the door of Daniella's private quarters and knocked.

"Oh, I was just going to find you," she said as she

appeared in the doorway. "Macy was wondering if you'd mind telling her good-night."

"Sure, I'll tell her good-night," he agreed. He followed her into Macy's bedroom, where Macy was already in bed.

Macy gave him a happy smile. "I wanted you to say good-night 'cause I had so much fun with you tonight."

"I had fun, too," Sam said as he sat on the edge of her bed.

"Mommy said you are going home in two days. Can't you please stay longer?"

"Macy!" Daniella said, obviously surprised by Macy's question.

Sam held up his hand to halt her protest and smiled at the little girl. "I can't, honey. I have to go back home and work. Remember I told you that I'm a monster hunter. It's a very important job."

"It would be an important job to stay here and be my friend, too," Macy countered.

Sam's heart squeezed tight in his chest as he leaned down and kissed Macy's forehead. "Sleep tight, princess," he said, and stood before his emotions could get away from him.

As he stepped out of Macy's room he took Daniella's arm. "I stepped outside on the porch a minute ago and found a box of candy and a coloring book there."

Her eyes darkened. "I know it's crazy, but I'd hoped it was over."

"This time I think he left you a note."

He wouldn't have thought it was possible for her eyes to grow darker, but they did. "A note?" Her voice was a whisper.

He nodded and together they went into the kitchen and to the table. She stared at the box of candy as if it were a poisonous snake ready to spring.

"Use the gloves," he said softly. "It's possible he left us some fingerprints. We'll get these things to Jim and he can print them. Maybe we'll get lucky."

"Luck doesn't seem to be in an abundant supply right now." She pulled on the gloves, moving in the slow motion of dread. She pulled the card loose from the box of candy and opened it. Sam moved to stand just behind her so he could see what the card contained.

"You belong to me."

The words were handwritten, printed in red ink. The word *me* was underlined with several strokes that had been so hard the pen had nearly torn through the paper.

Sam's stomach clenched. This was a definite escalation. First, the fact that there was contact made by the note, and second, the words and the emotion behind them were more than a statement. They were a definite threat.

Daniella threw down the card as if it had burned her through the plastic gloves. She turned around to look at Sam, and he saw the yawning horror in her eyes. "Who is doing this? Dammit, who could it be?"

"I'll call Jim," he said as he pulled his cell phone

from his pocket. "And, Daniella, I'm not going anywhere until this is all resolved."

The look she gave him was filled with gratitude. There was no way he could walk away now. He punched in Jim's number and as he waited for the sheriff to answer, he suspected it wasn't going to take weeks or months for this to all come to a head.

The note had been written with barely suppressed rage. Whoever had written it was reaching a breaking point. Sam had a feeling the explosion would happen within the next week or so. He just hoped that when it was over Daniella and Macy would be okay and he could finally walk away without looking back.

"You have a couple of big plastic food bags?" Jim asked as he eyed the box of chocolates and the coloring book on the table. "I didn't bring a kit with me. To tell the truth I don't do much fingerprinting personally anymore. But Deputy Wilkerson is a master at pulling prints off almost anything."

Daniella walked to the pantry, grateful that Jim had arrived quickly and intended to take the items with him. She didn't want them in the house, didn't even want them in the trash can outside of the house.

She retrieved two large bags and returned to the two men. Jim took the bags from her and, using his own pair of gloves, placed the candy box with the note in one and the coloring book in the other.

If there was one thing that told her how serious this latest turn of events was, it was the fact that Sam had decided to hang around longer than his intended visit. It both concerned her and relieved her.

"I know we've been over this before," Jim said. "But is there anyone you can think of who might be behind this? Somebody who has a crush on you, somebody who hangs around for no real reason?"

"Jim, I've thought and thought about this and I can't think of anyone."

"Jeff," Sam said. "Jeff Tyson has a thing for her."

Jim looked at Daniella. "What kind of a thing?"

"You know Jeff and Johnny were best friends. Since Johnny's disappearance Jeff has stepped in as a friend, a helpmate to me and Macy." She hesitated a moment and then continued. "Lately I've gotten the feeling that he might want something more from me."

"He's in love with her." Sam looked at her. "You know it's true." He returned his gaze to Jim. "He was here earlier this evening and got in a little pissing match with me, told me if I hurt Daniella he'll hunt me down and hurt me."

Daniella looked at him in surprise. "Jeff did that?" She was stunned and more than a little embarrassed. Jeff had no right to interfere with her personal life and she'd never seen that side of him before.

"I don't like the sound of that," Jim said with a frown. "Look, Daniella, I know you and I had a rough go of it when Johnny disappeared, but I promise you I'm doing everything I can to solve Samantha's murder and find who attacked you. There's no question in my mind that the two crimes are tied together, that your stalker thought he was doing you a favor by killing Samantha."

"So I don't need a criminal defense lawyer?" she asked.

"You never really did," Jim replied. He picked up the plastic bags. "I'll let you know if we manage to pull any prints off these things. In the meantime watch your back and let me know if anything else comes up."

Sam walked Jim to the front door as Daniella sank down in a chair at the table. Matt and Jeff, secrets and lies. Murder and stalking. What had happened to her ordinary life?

She couldn't believe that Jeff had threatened Sam. She found that just as difficult to swallow as the possibility that Matt might have had something to do with his wife's death.

She felt as if her entire world had been turned upside down, twisted inside out, and she didn't know how to make it right again.

Sam walked back into the kitchen, his gaze dark and unreadable. "Maybe he got careless and left prints all over those things."

"And the Easter bunny is on his way with chocolate eggs for everyone," she said dryly. "I've got a house-ful of people arriving first thing Saturday morning and somebody dangerous who wants to make me his own." She rubbed the center of her forehead where a headache attempted to blossom into full bloom.

"Go to bed, Daniella. Nothing more can be done tonight. I'll let you know in the morning if I hear from

Jim. I told him to call me with the fingerprint results. Just go to bed. I'll make sure everything is locked up tight."

She nodded wearily and got up from the table, too exhausted to talk anymore. "Thanks, Sam. I'll see you in the morning."

Minutes later, in the privacy of her room, she changed into her nightgown and tried not to think about everything that was happening.

She shouldn't have been thinking about obsession and murder, she thought. Instead she should have been focused on weekend menus and how to make sure her guests had a lovely experience staying with her.

Although she was grateful that Sam had decided to extend his stay, she knew it was only going to make it more difficult when it came time to tell him goodbye.

She was in love with him. It hit her like a fist to the chest, leaving her nearly breathless. Somehow, some way in the past two weeks she'd fallen head over heels with the Prince of Darkness.

And he was going to break her heart.

She got into bed and squeezed her eyes tightly closed. She didn't want to think about telling Sam goodbye. Losing Johnny had been devastating, but she'd eventually healed. She had a feeling that losing Sam would be even more difficult to get over.

She fell asleep and dreamed of monsters and Macy in her princess crown, trying to banish bad men with a wave of her wand. She awoke at dawn, feeling as exhausted as she had when she'd gone to sleep.

Showered and dressed, she checked on Macy, who was still sound asleep, then went into the kitchen to get some coffee brewing.

She was standing at the window, staring out and sipping a cup of coffee, when Matt came into the kitchen. Since she'd learned about the fact that he had been a suspect in his wife's death there was no question that she felt a bit uneasy around him, although she'd tried to hide it from him.

"You're up early," she said as she tried to ignore the small knot of tension that formed in her stomach.

"Yeah, I'm heading over to the house before going into the office. I just wanted to let you know that the builder has assured me that I should be able to take possession in two weeks, so I guess I'll be out of here then."

"Thanks for the heads-up." She took a sip of her coffee and made a quick, impulsive decision. "Matt, you never told me how your wife died. Was she ill?"

His eyes darkened as he leaned against the doorjamb. "No, not ill. She was perfectly healthy when she died. I was in the living room when she told me she was going to go into the bathroom and clean out the tub, then take a nice, long bath."

He paused a moment and it was obvious he was reining in emotions. "I don't know exactly what happened. After about an hour I realized she was taking too long. I went into the bathroom and found her sprawled in the tub. Her head was bloody and she was dead. She must have slipped. She was still dressed and the bottle of cleaner was in the tub with her." He pulled a hand down his face. "Cindy's death was a nightmare, but the nightmare went on when the police told me they thought I'd killed her."

Daniella gasped as if she didn't already know the story. "Why would they think that?"

"Cindy and I were going through a rough patch. We were financially overextended, and because of the stress we were fighting about stupid stuff. We weren't headed for a divorce—we loved each other. But when you're in the middle of an investigation things get magnified and blown out of proportion."

"I'm sorry, Matt." She saw the grief in his eyes, and she didn't know if she was being too gullible, but she believed him.

"You know what the worst part is? With each step of building this house I've thought about her. When I put the island in the kitchen I thought about how excited Cindy would have been. She'd always wanted an island in the kitchen, and then I remembered she'd never see this house. She'd never cook in the kitchen. She'd never walk down the hallways."

At that moment Sam appeared and Matt seemed to pull himself together. "Good morning," he said to Sam. "I was just telling Daniella that the builder has told me I should be able to move into my new place in two weeks."

"Congratulations," Sam said as he moved past Matt to the coffeemaker.

Minutes later Matt had left and Daniella and Sam

sat at the kitchen table. "He told me all about his wife's death, that it was a tragic accident," Daniella said. "I felt such pain in him as he was telling me. I believe him, Sam."

He smiled. "I think it's a good thing you aren't a cop. You're definitely an easy touch."

"Maybe," she agreed. "But even if Matt had something to do with his wife's death, I can't imagine what that might have to do with what's happening now. Matt isn't harboring some sort of secret obsession for me."

"Maybe you'd be surprised by who is obsessing over you," he replied, and although his tone was light, his gaze was warm as it lingered on her.

You, Sam? she wanted to ask. *Do you obsess about me just a little bit?*

"You're the kind of woman plenty of men might obsess about," he continued. "You're beautiful and soft and loving." He leaned forward slightly, his gaze focused on her lips, and for a moment she thought he might kiss her—she wanted him to kiss her. Anticipation shot a wave of warmth through her.

He straightened and broke the eye contact. "But there's no question that somebody has a sick, dark obsession with you."

"I can't help but think that if that were true I'd know, I'd feel it."

The light that had been in his eyes only seconds before diminished as he once again looked at her. "That's the thing about the darkness, Daniella. You can't see the monsters that hide in the shadows."

"Then everyone should be as lucky as me and have an FBI agent staying beneath their roof," she replied, but she couldn't stop the chill that slid through her at his words.

Chapter Nine

By Friday afternoon Sam felt the need to get out of the house. Daniella had been busy all day preparing for the onslaught of guests the next morning. Sam had even gotten in on the act, helping her change the sheets on the beds in the carriage house while Macy dusted the furniture.

"Why don't we take off an hour or two and take a little ride to town?" he said to the two of them after lunch was finished.

Daniella looked at him in surprise at the same time Macy clapped her hands together in delight. "Why?" Daniella asked. "Is there something you need from town?"

"I just thought it might be nice to walk around a little bit, maybe get a piece of pie at the café." What he wanted to do was get away from the house that smelled of her, where he'd have something else to think about besides how badly he wanted her again.

"Come on, Mommy, let's go. I love pie at the café," Macy exclaimed.

Daniella frowned. "I still have so many things to do here."

"An hour," Sam replied. "Just take an hour off."

"Yeah, an hour," Macy said pleadingly.

"You two are a bad influence on a working woman," Daniella exclaimed. "Macy, go brush your hair and I'll go get my purse."

Minutes later the three of them left Frank in charge of the house, and they were in Sam's car headed into town. "Maybe we could go into the discount store and I could get a new outfit for my Barbie doll," Macy said.

"I'm not sure shopping for fashion doll clothing is what Sam had in mind," Daniella replied.

Sam smiled. "Actually it was exactly what I had in mind." He glanced at Daniella, who looked as pretty as he'd ever seen her in a sunshine-yellow blouse and white shorts. "I just thought we needed a little outing after the last few days."

"I have to admit, it feels good to be out," she replied.

If Sam had hoped that the outing would somehow diminish his desire for Daniella, he was sadly mistaken. Once they arrived in town he parked the car, and the three of them went into the discount store to find Macy the perfect outfit for her doll.

As he watched mother and daughter interacting over the purchase, he was rocked by the desire not just to have Daniella in his bed, but to have her and Macy in his life. Their laughter filled his heart and fed his soul.

They left the discount store after Macy had found the

perfect beautiful dress for her doll, then walked around the square and finally wound up in the café, where they took a booth and ordered pie.

"It's not as good as yours," Macy said to Daniella after the first bite of her chocolate cream pie. "Does your mom make pies, Mr. Sam?"

"No, honey. My mom is in heaven."

Macy's eyes softened. "Oh, that's sad. Did you love your mommy as much as I love mine?"

Sam hadn't thought about his mother in a very long time. It was always his father the monster that consumed his thoughts. "Yes, I did."

"What was she like?" Daniella asked curiously.

"Quiet and kind." Memories began to tumble around in his head, pleasant memories that warmed him. "She didn't ask for much and seemed happiest spending time with me. She was a homemaker. She loved to take care of us."

His stomach clenched as he thought of how her life had been taken so abruptly, so brutally.

"She never considered leaving your father?" Daniella asked.

"If she did I didn't know about it," he replied. "I think she kept hoping he would become the man she wanted him to be."

"Mr. Sam, I'm glad you decided not to leave today," Macy said, and Sam was relieved for the change in topic.

"But you understand I'm going to be leaving soon," Sam replied.

Macy put her fingers in her ears. "La-la-la, I can't hear you."

Sam laughed and knew that whenever he left here, a small piece of his heart would remain behind with the precocious little girl.

"What about your parents?" he asked Daniella.

"My father died when I was six, so it was just my mother and I." She paused to take a sip of her soda and then continued. "My mom was a lot like your mother. She was kindhearted, and even though we didn't have much she made me feel rich in so many ways."

"And how did she die?"

"When I was a junior in high school she was diagnosed with an aggressive liver cancer. She saw me graduate and marry Johnny, and then she passed away."

"Did she like Johnny?" he asked.

Daniella smiled. "Adored him. Everyone loved Johnny."

"But he got lost," Macy said sadly. "And I don't think he's ever coming back."

"Someday maybe your mommy will fall in love with a nice man who will make you a wonderful father," Sam said, surprised by how much he hated the idea of the two of them building a life together with another man.

"Maybe that could be you," Macy said with a sly look at him.

"Macy, don't start," Daniella said in a warning voice as her cheeks grew pink.

"But, Mommy, I already love Mr. Sam, and I know if you try really hard you could love him, too," Macy replied. "I thought he was going to be a cranky-pants at first, but he put on his big-girl pants and got over that."

This time it was Sam's turn to feel his face warm as Daniella laughed. "I'd like to see you in those big-girl pants," she said under her breath.

They finished up their pie. But Sam hadn't lost track of the fact that somebody was after Daniella. He had eyed each and every person that looked their way, kept them close to his side as they'd walked the streets.

He was a man enjoying a woman's company, but he also didn't forget that he was an FBI agent trying to keep that woman safe.

When they left the café they made a final walk into the center square where the statue of the town founder and the legend of Bachelor Moon lived.

"You're a brave man to stand there," Daniella observed, as Sam stood before the statue.

He grinned at her. "Not so brave at all. Notice I'm standing here with the full moon still a week away."

Daniella laughed and then sobered. "We really should get back. I've still got a lot of work to do for the weekend. The guests will be arriving around noon."

"I can't wait to call Lisa and tell her I got a beautiful dress for my doll," Macy said, once they were back in the car and headed home. "Maybe she could spend the night tonight?"

"Not tonight, honey," Daniella replied. "Maybe one night next week after our weekenders leave."

Was it possible one of the guests for the weekend was

the person they sought? There was nothing to say that the man was from Bachelor Moon. He frowned at this new thought.

"Any of the people coming this weekend repeat guests?" he asked casually.

"No. Why?"

He felt her curious gaze on him. "Just wondering."

"I'm not sure I believe that you just wonder about anything without a reason," she countered.

"I think maybe we should have this conversation another time." He looked pointedly in the rearview mirror to where Macy sat.

It didn't take long after they got home for them to have the conversation. Macy was in her bedroom playing with her dolls. Daniella joined Sam in the kitchen, where they seemed to spend a lot of their time together.

"What are you thinking, Sam?" she asked.

He sat at the table while she got out the things she needed to make cinnamon rolls for the morning. "I just wondered if maybe we've been wrong in suspecting it's somebody close to you here. Maybe the man who is after you stayed here at some time in the past. Maybe he lives someplace close enough that he could drive in to leave his gifts for you."

She measured flour into a bowl and then turned to face him. "Most of my guests so far have been from out of state."

"But there have been some who have stayed here that live within driving distance?"

"I can think of a few, but I'd have to check my records."

"Could you do that later this evening?"

"I'll make a point of it," she said, and turned back around to her task.

For the next two hours Sam drank lemonade and watched her as she prepared a variety of food for the weekend. He liked watching her work. He enjoyed the way a tiny wrinkle creased her forehead when she was in deep concentration, how she occasionally smiled to herself when she was pleased with the results of whatever it was she was doing.

Their conversation was light, the kind that two people who had just begun dating might have—favorite foods and movies, stories from their youths, and local people and places.

He could be happy here, he thought. If he believed in real happiness. But Sam had stopped believing in happiness the day that his mother had died, the day his father had tried to kill him.

It was after Macy was in bed for the night that they sat down together at the table to look over her records of previous guests. "When we first opened the doors, I remember that several local people booked for a night just to see what it was all about."

As she leaned forward over the paperwork her hair fell forward, a sheet of golden shine that made his fingers itch with the need to touch.

When he could stand it no longer he reached out and tucked the errant strand behind her ear. She looked up and smiled gratefully then focused again on the papers.

In that moment Sam felt oddly vulnerable, half crazy with emotions he'd never felt before and knew he would never feel again.

Focus, he told himself firmly. The only reason he'd decided to stay here was for her safety and nothing else. Within a few days of leaving here he'd be back immersed in his job, back into the darkness that had in many ways become comfortably familiar.

DANIELLA FELT A STRANGE energy wafting from Sam as she finally came up with the names of the people who had visited the bed-and-breakfast and lived within driving distance.

She assumed his thoughts centered on trying to figure out who might be the man in the shadows who was threatening her. She also wondered if he was regretting his decision to stay longer than he'd anticipated.

There was no question that he was putting his life on hold for her, and although she was grateful for his presence, she also felt more than a little bit guilty.

"Matt James and his wife, Damon Cole and his girlfriend, Susan Boyd and her boyfriend, James." She leaned back in her chair. "Those are the people who have visited here and live within driving distance, but I can't imagine any of those men focusing some sort of sick obsession on me."

"Why not? You're beautiful and sexy. You have a

great sense of humor, and any man would be a fool not to be attracted to you."

His words stunned her and made her wonder in the depths of her heart why he couldn't love her enough to throw caution to the wind, to forget that at some point in his life he'd decided to live his life alone.

"I appreciate the nice words, but it doesn't change the fact that I can't believe any of these men are responsible for what's been happening." She looked down at her records once again. "Besides, the gifts started arriving before Matt James and Damon Cole even visited here."

She sighed. "We're spinning our wheels, Sam. We have to face the fact that we don't have a clue who this man is or why he's focused his attention on me, and the truth of the matter is that it might take weeks or months for us to finally figure it out."

Her heart beat the rhythm of dread. "Sam, I don't want to keep you from your life. I don't want you here because of some strange sense of duty you might feel toward me."

What she wanted was him to be here because he couldn't stand the thought of leaving her, because he'd fallen in love with her as she had with him.

There had been times when she'd thought she'd seen something like love in his eyes when he looked at her, times when he touched her as if unable to stop himself.

"Daniella, I'm still here because I want to be. It's more than duty. I care about you and Macy."

"And I'm in love with you." The words blurted out of her. He winced, and she quickly looked down at the table, both embarrassed and oddly relieved by the confession.

There was a long silence and when she could stand it no longer she looked back at him, her heart beating faster than usual.

He cleared his throat as if uncomfortable. His eyes were as distant as the stars in the sky, impossible to read as he leaned forward. "Daniella, I think maybe you think you love me because I've been the only one you can trust, because you've been going through a bad time and I've been there for you."

She shook her head, unsurprised that he'd attempted to somehow justify and minimize her feelings for him. "Sam, I know what love feels like. I know how it tastes in my mouth, how it feels inside my skin. I know love, and I know that I'm in love with you."

He held her gaze for a long moment and then released a weary sigh and ran a hand through his hair. "I didn't mean for that to happen. I didn't want that to happen. Maybe Jeff was right. Maybe I took advantage of you."

"Don't be ridiculous," she scoffed. "You didn't take advantage of me. I'm a big girl. I made my decisions about you based on what I wanted, what I needed. I didn't expect to fall in love with you, but I did. And I guess I just wanted you to know how I felt."

"You know it doesn't change anything." His voice was

deep, his tone holding an apology. "I'm still leaving here. I never intend to marry. I don't want a relationship."

"Why not?" She wanted to understand, needed to understand what would forever keep him alone in his life. "Even if it's not me? Why not somebody else?"

His eyes grew dark and a knot pulsed in his jaw. "It doesn't matter why I've made the decision. It is what it is and it isn't going to change. I'm sorry if I led you on."

She shook her head, feeling a heavy weight where her heart should have been. "You know you didn't. You've been up front with me about everything from the very beginning. I'd just hoped..." She allowed her voice to trail off.

"I'm sorry." His voice was husky with emotion.

Her heart fell to her feet. Until this moment she hadn't realized that she'd entertained a wild hope that somehow, someway, they'd end up together. Now that hope had been stripped from her, and she felt slightly sick.

"I think on that note it's time for me to call it a day," she said, suddenly eager to escape him. She got up from the table and gathered her papers. He halted her by placing his hand on her forearm. His very touch hurt. Because she wanted it, because she wanted him.

"I'm sorry, Daniella. I'm so damned sorry."

She forced a smile and pulled her arm away. "Don't worry about it. It's my problem, not yours, and I'll be fine." She raised her chin a notch. "I'm always fine. I'll see you in the morning."

Don't be a crybaby, she told herself as she left the

kitchen and went into her private rooms. There was absolutely nothing to cry about. He'd been a guest who got too close, an FBI agent she'd depended on, and when he left she'd be okay.

Still, she couldn't halt the sting of tears that burned her eyes as she stood in the doorway to Macy's room. It was just her luck that she'd first fallen in love with a man who decided not to stick around—or couldn't—and then made the mistake again of falling for another man who *wouldn't* stick around.

It had been unrealistic of her to even think there might be a happy ending in store for her. Even if Sam was in the market for a relationship with her, he was in Kansas City and she was in Louisiana. She could never ask him to leave his work and relocate here, and she would be reluctant to uproot Macy from this place that was so deep in Daniella's heart.

She turned away from Macy's bedroom and went into her own, where she sat on the bed and stared blankly at the wall. She shouldn't have told him how she felt, but there had been a little piece of her that had thought maybe he'd jump out of his chair and pull her into his arms and tell her he loved her, too.

She had one man she wished was just a little bit obsessed with her and another who was dangerously over-the-top obsessed with her. Sometimes life was just a crazy ride.

Weary and more than a little bit heartbroken, she changed into her nightgown and got into bed. Tomorrow, hopefully, she would be too busy with the new guests to even think about Sam or love or anything else.

She squeezed her eyes closed tightly. She wanted her life back, the life where she didn't have to worry about some demented person wanting her, the life where her heart was fully guarded against any invasion by a man.

Sleep. She just wanted to sleep and forget for now how badly her heart hurt.

She was dreaming about Sam, the weight of his body on top of her, his lips pressed against her own. The pleasant dream transformed as his weight on top of her pressed harder and she realized she couldn't breathe.

It was then she woke up but her brain screamed as she realized the sensations she'd felt in the dream were real. Somebody was on top of her and a hand was pressing a cloth over her nose. The cloth was big enough to cover her entire face and panic arced through her.

She tried to scream but the cloth was so tight against her nose and mouth the sound was muffled. The heavy weight on top of her made it impossible for her to escape.

Help me! Her brain screamed the words as she tried to flail her arms, tried to move her legs. She held her breath, knowing that any air she drew in would be poisonous.

They'd thought she would be safe in the house, in her own room. She'd never considered that danger could get to her here.

Sam and Matt were just up the stairs, Macy was in the other room.

Macy. Oh, God, don't let anything happen to Macy.

Daniella could hold her breath no longer. Her air-deprived lungs screamed in agony. She didn't want to breathe, knew that when she did she'd be lost.

Just like Johnny.

Never to be seen again.

Tears burned her eyes as she finally drew in a breath and then another and then another and then she was lost.

Chapter Ten

Sam awoke before dawn but was reluctant to get up and face Daniella. One of the most difficult things he'd ever been through was listening to her profess her love for him and then having to break her heart.

And he had broken her heart. He'd seen it in her eyes, heard it in her voice when she'd finally told him good-night.

He should have never slept with her. He should have never spent time with her other than what was necessary as a guest in her house. He'd involved himself not only in the crimes that were taking place here, but also in Daniella's and Macy's lives, and that had been his biggest mistake.

Finally getting out of bed, he stood beneath the spray of a hot shower, his thoughts racing in a thousand different directions.

Macy wanted him as her new daddy, and a part of him would have loved that role in her life. But she deserved better.

Daniella deserved better than him, as well. The best

thing he could do for both of them was remain firm in leaving here. And maybe it was time for him to go.

He shut off the water and grabbed the towel, and as he dried off he considered his options. He'd told Daniella he'd remain here until the danger had passed, but he'd made that decision in the heat of the moment when she'd received the card from the unsub. Unidentified subject.

Who in the hell was behind all this? And how long would it be before he was caught?

Maybe the best thing he could do for Daniella and Macy was leave now, before the emotions got even messier. Despite whatever baggage had once been between the sheriff and Daniella, Sam felt confident that Jim was doing everything in his power.

He could even hire a professional bodyguard to stay here for the duration, he thought, as he dressed and headed downstairs. He knew a couple of retired agents that would jump at the chance for some extra cash.

As he reached the bottom of the stairs he frowned as he realized he didn't smell coffee. A check of his watch let him know it was almost seven. Daniella always had the coffee brewing by now.

Walking through toward the kitchen he glanced out the window and saw Frank in the distance weeding one of the flower beds.

It was like any other day, except Sam didn't smell the coffee, and that concerned him just a little bit. He went into the kitchen and saw that it didn't appear as if Daniella had been there that morning.

The door to her private quarters was closed. Was she reluctant to face him this morning? No. Daniella wasn't the kind of woman to hide in her room. Maybe she'd overslept? He didn't believe that either, not on a morning when new guests were arriving.

Maybe she was sick? Or maybe Macy was ill. Whatever was going on, it was out of the ordinary and Sam didn't like it. He turned at the sound of a knock on the back door. Frank waved to him through the window.

"Morning," Frank said when Sam had unlocked the door and allowed him inside.

"Morning to you," Sam replied. "Have you seen Daniella around?"

"No. I went straight out to that flower bed this morning and didn't come to the house until now." He frowned as he looked at the empty coffeepot. "Is she sick or something?"

"I'm about to find out," Sam said as he walked toward her door. He knocked on it and waited for a response. Nothing. He knocked again, this time more forcefully. "Daniella," he called.

When there was still no reply a thick tension coiled tight in Sam's stomach. He tried the doorknob but it was locked. He bent down and looked to see that it was an ordinary interior door lock often used on bathrooms.

"Frank, get me something sharp," he demanded, as he tried to quell the panic that attempted to roar through him. He rapped frantically on the door, the resulting silence screaming in his head.

Frank returned with a tiny screwdriver that Sam

maneuvered into the tiny hole next to the knob. His heart beat fast and furious as he popped the lock and opened the door.

The silence inside the room was hollow, as if no living creatures existed inside the space and Sam didn't linger but raced toward Daniella's bedroom.

He stopped in the doorway, his heart crashing to the floor as he saw her empty bed. It was obvious she'd slept there; the covers were rumpled and the pillow still held the depression from her head. So where was she?

He shoved Frank out of the way and ran toward Macy's room. Macy's bed was empty, as well, the covers on one side hanging to the floor, as if her little body had been dragged from the bed.

The window next to the bed was open, the screen removed, and the sight nearly overwhelmed Sam. "Call the sheriff," he said to Frank, his throat nearly constricted with emotion.

It was horrifyingly easy to assess what had happened. Somebody had come in through the window and had managed to spirit away both Daniella and Macy.

As Frank left, the illness that filled Sam nearly cast him to his knees. He'd thought they were safe in the house. He'd believed that the monster couldn't get to them here.

God, he should have been more vigilant. He should have been sleeping on the sofa in Daniella's private quarters. He should never have let them out of his sight. Now they were gone, and he didn't know where to begin to look for them, was afraid to hazard a guess as to if they were alive or dead.

"Jim's on his way," Frank said as he rejoined Sam in the doorway of Macy's room. "What do you think happened to them?"

"I don't know...something bad." Sam felt as if he couldn't catch his breath as he gazed at the bed covered with pink sheets and ruffles.

The focus had seemed to be on Daniella, so why was Macy missing, as well? The toys. Sam hadn't thought about the toys that had been left as gifts. The perp had wanted both Daniella and Macy.

"Don't touch anything," he said to Frank. "Let's wait for Jim in the kitchen."

Sam didn't want to stand around and wait for anything or anyone, but he also didn't want to contaminate what he assumed was a crime scene.

Matt. Was he here?

At this thought Sam ran out of the kitchen and took the stairs two at a time. He raced down the hallway, and when he reached the door to Matt's room he banged his fist against it in a frantic tattoo.

If Matt had anything to do with hurting Daniella or Macy, Sam would kill him. There would be no arrest, no due process for him.

Sam banged on the door again and was surprised to hear Matt. "Okay, okay. I'm coming."

He opened the door, and all the wind inside Sam whooshed out. Matt was clad in a bathrobe and half his face was covered in shaving cream. "What are you trying to do, bust down my door?"

"Daniella and Macy are missing."

Matt frowned. "Missing? What do you mean missing?"

"They've been kidnapped." Sam knew the answer wasn't here with Matt. It was one of those gut feelings that he'd always relied on.

"Kidnapped?" Matt's jaw dropped and he looked at Sam with incomprehension. "Kidnapped from here? When?"

"Sometime last night." Sam backed away from the door. "Jim is on his way. I've got to get back downstairs."

Once downstairs again Sam paced the kitchen floor. He was a man of action, a man who investigated crimes. He wasn't used to cooling his heels in the heat of the moment.

And there was no question in his mind that this was the heat of the moment, that if Daniella and Macy were still alive their lives were at risk and time might be running out.

Unable to stay cooped up any longer, he told Frank he'd be right back, then left the house by the front door and walked around to the open window in Macy's room.

He scanned the area with narrowed eyes, looking for something, anything that might provide a clue. The ground was too hard to show any footprints, and he saw nothing that might have been dropped or left behind by the perpetrator.

Jim found him there, the older man's expression grim. "They're gone, Jim. Somebody got them." Sam's voice was hollow, thick with the emotion he was trying desperately to tamp down.

"Frank told me. We're going to find them, Sam. I've got Deputy Wilkerson inside starting the fingerprinting of the rooms."

"I want you to send some men over to Matt Rader's new home and see if they find anything there."

Jim raised a grizzly eyebrow. "You think he had something to do with this?"

"Not really, but I'd never forgive myself if I was wrong in my assessment." Sam's stomach twisted in knots. He reached out and grabbed Jim by the shoulder. "We have to find them. This kind of obsession can be dangerous, explosive." He dropped his hand back to his side.

"You didn't hear anything last night? No scream? No struggle? No car pulling up out front?"

Sam shook his head. "Nothing. And I'm a light sleeper." A cold wind blew through Sam despite the rising heat of the day. "There wasn't a struggle in the bedrooms. Whoever did this managed to get them out of the house without a struggle."

He frowned, his thoughts once again racing. "They had to have been drugged. It's the only thing that explains why there was no struggle, why there wasn't a scream."

"Let's go back inside and see if Wilkerson has managed to lift some prints or if there's something the creep left behind," Jim said.

When they returned to the house they found Frank in the common room. The older man looked as sick as Sam felt. "Anything?" he asked hopefully.

Sam shook his head.

"I was wondering if it would be okay if I went into the kitchen and checked on the meal plans Daniella had for the weekend. We've got guests coming in around noon, and I know she'd want to keep everything as normal as possible for them." Frank looked from Sam to Jim.

"I don't have a problem with that," Jim said.

"I'm sure Daniella would appreciate it," Sam added.

Frank shrugged. "That's what I do, I take care of things for Daniella. I'll hold the fort here. You two just figure out how to find her and Macy."

As he left the room in the direction of the kitchen, Sam turned back to Jim. "You take care of things here. I've got someplace to go."

"Want to tell me where you're going?" Jim asked.

"I'm following a hunch," Sam replied.

"Want to share with me?"

Sam shook his head. "You'll know if it pans out because you'll be arresting me for murder." Sam turned and left before Jim could stop him.

THE HEADACHE PULLED HER from sleep, a nauseating pounding at the temples that made her stomach roll.

Daniella kept her eyes closed as consciousness slowly came. The bed was soft and warm, and she was reluctant to start her day until the headache abated somewhat.

At least she had everything ready for the new guests who would be arriving. Their rooms were clean and inviting, and she'd done a lot of the cooking in advance.

The one thing she didn't want to think about was her conversation with Sam. Then she wouldn't only have a headache, but her heart would hurt, as well.

She turned over and her elbow hit a wall. A wall? She frowned. That was impossible in her bed. Her eyes snapped open and she sat up, ignoring the pound of her head as she looked over her surroundings.

Horrifying shock gripped her, along with a cascade of memories from the night before. The heavy weight on her body, the cloth shoved tight against her face, each and every moment of the horrifying ordeal came slamming back into her brain.

Where was she? She was in a bed, shoved against a wall in a large, windowless room. An electric bulb dangled from a wire in the drop ceiling over a small kitchen table and provided enough light for her to see.

There was a sofa and a chair, a refrigerator and a microwave and a sink. Like a tiny apartment, it contained everything somebody would need to survive.

The only sound was the faint hum of the refrigerator. There were three doors, all closed. The one at the end of the room she assumed led outside.

At the moment her fear was tamped down, simmering beneath the surface but not screaming out loud. Who had brought her here? Who had crept into her room and then carried her out of it when she was unconscious?

She slid her legs over the side of the bed and put her feet on the slightly uneven linoleum floor. Cold. She was so cold, and she suspected she might be in some sort of shock.

Headache forgotten, she walked toward the nearest door. It opened to a small bathroom with a stand-up shower. She leaned against the door as a tremor worked through her, the force of it nearly buckling her knees.

This place was nothing more than a slightly upscale jail cell. She was a prisoner here. Out. She had to get out! She ran to the next door and twisted the knob, but found it locked with a padlock. The third door was locked, as well. She rattled and pulled, but the doors were solid and she knew she was simply expending her energy for nothing.

A sob escaped her as she crawled back to the bed. She scrambled into the corner, her back against the wall, and drew her legs up to her chest.

The monster had her and she was now in his lair. What were his intentions? What did he want from her? She didn't even know if she was still in the town of Bachelor Moon. She could be a hundred miles away from home, from Macy.

Macy.

Her heart ripped at thoughts of her daughter. Surely Sam and Frank would take care of her baby while she was gone. And she'd be home before she knew it. Somehow Sam would find her. That's what he did; he found the monsters and destroyed them.

She squeezed her eyes tightly closed as another sob ripped through her. What if she never saw Macy again? What if she remained imprisoned here until she died?

The thought of never again smelling the sweet scent of her daughter, of never again holding her in her arms, overwhelmed her with grief.

Deep sobs tore up her throat as she pulled her legs more tightly against her chest. Who had done this? Who had broken into her room in the middle of the night to take her prisoner?

The sobs only lasted a minute. *Think,* she commanded herself. *Think about how you can get out of here.* She couldn't wait for Sam to ride to her rescue; she had to try to do something to save herself.

She uncurled from the corner and got to her feet. The cabinet beneath the microwave held water glasses and plates, but only plastic silverware—nothing that could be used to pry at a door.

"Dammit!" The word released from her on a scream.

"Mommy?"

Daniella froze, wondering if Macy's voice was only wistful thinking in her head. "Mommy, are you out there?"

This time Daniella's heart clenched as she realized the voice was coming from the one of the doors she couldn't open. She raced to the door and sank to her knees.

"Macy, honey. I'm here." She pressed her hands against the door, as if by sheer willpower alone she could feel her baby girl. "Where are you?"

"I'm in a room," Macy replied.

"What kind of a room? Does it have a window?" Daniella fought against the horror of knowing her daughter was with her in this dangerous situation.

"No. It doesn't have a window, but it's a pretty room, kind of like mine at home. And there are toys and books on a shelf."

The words caused a new horror to sweep through Daniella. So whoever had taken her had planned on taking Macy, as well, had prepared for the little girl to be a prisoner, too.

"Can't you come in here with me, Mommy?"

"I can't, baby. The door is locked and I can't get in. Are you hurt?"

"No. I'm just a little bit scared and I have a headache," Macy replied.

Rage consumed Daniella, a rage directed at the man who was keeping her from her frightened, hurting child. She'd kill him if she got the chance, for no other reason than this.

"Macy, did you see who brought us here?" Daniella pressed closer against the door, wishing she could pass right through the wood.

"No. I was sleeping and then I woke up here. Mommy, what's happening?"

"It's an adventure, baby. I need you to be strong for

me. Don't be scared and very soon we'll be home and back together again." Daniella prayed that the words she spoke through the door to her daughter weren't empty ones.

Chapter Eleven

Sam clenched the steering wheel as he raced down the lane that led away from the bed-and-breakfast. It would take time for Jim and his deputies to thoroughly process the crime scenes in Daniella's and Macy's bedrooms. Frank was holding the fort for the guests to arrive, and there was no way Sam could just stand around and cool his heels when he knew the two people he loved most in the world were in trouble.

What had he missed? Nobody was as good as the perpetrator had been so far. There were almost always mistakes made and clues to be followed.

There was only one person on his radar, and he was on his way to confront him now. His only hope was that the person who had Daniella and Macy was still in the love phase of his obsession. But Sam knew how quickly in cases like this love could turn to rage, and that terrified him more than anything.

His father had professed to love his mother and him, but that hadn't stopped him from shooting his mother to death and attempting to do the same to Sam.

One of the pieces of information he'd gotten from

Lexie was the addresses of the people he'd asked her to background-search. Jeff's address was in Sam's head, and that was where he was headed.

Had Jeff entertained an obsession with Daniella? Had he fallen in love with his best friend's wife and had that crazy love prompted him to kill Johnny? Had the gifts to Macy and flowers to Daniella been part of a long and twisted courtship?

It was possible that Sam's relationship with Daniella had been what had forced Jeff to finally act in a more aggressive manner.

Sam slowed as he entered the town and looked at the street signs, searching for Walnut Street. The tension inside him twisted tighter with each second that passed.

What if it was already too late?

He tightened his grip on the steering wheel, refusing to allow those kinds of thought entry into his head.

He had to find them and they had to be okay. Any other outcome was absolutely unthinkable. He spied Walnut Street and made a left turn, then slowed to a crawl as he looked for Jeff's house.

Myriad emotions rumbled in his chest—fear and anger mixed with hope and despair. And above all of them a burn of urgency that had him half sick.

Jeff's house was an attractive two-story painted a pale green with beige shutters at the windows. A large porch held several pots of brightly colored flowers, and Jeff's car was in the driveway.

Sam parked behind it and got out, his blood running

hot in his veins. Before he'd left the bed-and-breakfast he'd grabbed his gun and he now tucked it in his waistband.

He took the stairs to the porch two at a time, and when he reached the front door he banged on it with his fist. It was just after eight. He assumed Jeff went into his office about nine. The man should be home getting ready for work, or perhaps he intended to take the day off to enjoy his new guests.

With this thought in mind, Sam banged against the door with all the force of a desperate man. He heard a voice call from inside, although it was muffled enough so he wasn't sure what was said.

As the door finally opened Sam placed a hand on the butt of his gun. Jeff stared at him in surprise through the screen door. He was clad in a bathrobe and his hair was mussed as if he'd just now climbed out of bed.

"Late night?" Sam asked.

"What are you doing here?" Jeff made no move to open the screen door that separated them.

"I need to search your house. You here alone?"

Jeff stared at him for another minute and then laughed and shook his head. "I am, not that it's any of your business. And you sure as hell aren't coming in here without a search warrant. What exactly is it that you're looking for?"

"Daniella and Macy." Their very names ached falling from his lips.

Jeff narrowed his eyes, threw a glance over his shoulder and then stepped out on the porch. "What in the hell are you talking about?"

"They're gone, kidnapped from the bed-and-breakfast sometime last night. I intend to search your house with or without your permission." Sam pulled the gun, knowing in some small place of his brain that he'd gone around the bend, was half crazy with his fear.

"Sam, you're wasting your time," Jeff said, his eyes dark with worry. "I had nothing to do with this. They aren't here, I swear to you."

"Seeing is believing. Step away from the door, Jeff. I don't want to have to hurt you."

Jeff must have sensed the barely suppressed rage inside Sam. Sam hadn't missed the quick over-the-shoulder glance Jeff had given before stepping out on the porch. Sam knew with a gut certainty that there was somebody else in the house.

For a long moment the two men stared at each other and finally Jeff stepped away from the door. "I don't want a scandal," Jeff said as Sam entered the house.

Sam didn't give a damn what Jeff wanted or didn't want. All he needed was to find Daniella and Macy and get them home where they belonged.

He'd only just entered the living room when he heard the creak of floorboards from upstairs. Were they up there locked in a room? Unable to get out or call for help?

His heart crashed against his ribs as he raced up the stairs. He didn't give a damn if Jeff tried to make a run for it. They would find him wherever he tried to hide.

At the moment all that was important was getting to Daniella and Macy.

At the top of the stairs he saw that all the doors to the bedrooms were opened except one, and it was to that one that he ran.

He threw open the door and froze in stunned surprise. Tina from the café squealed in surprise from the bed where she lay. She clutched the sheet up to her bare chest, her cheeks pink with embarrassment.

Sam nearly fell to his knees in disappointment. "Were you here all night?" His voice sounded hoarse, alien to his own ears.

She nodded, her eyes wide as she saw the gun in his hand. "What are you doing in here?"

"Nothing." He tucked the gun back in his waistband and headed down the stairs where Jeff stood at the front door.

"Tina and I had a few drinks last night," Jeff said. "Things kind of got out of control. I would prefer you not mention this to anyone. This is a small town, and I don't want people thinking less of Tina."

"I've got to get out of here," Sam replied. Emotion tore up the back of his throat.

"You'll let me know about Daniella and Macy?" Jeff asked.

Sam nodded and then hurried to his car. He pulled out of the driveway and down the block and a cold wind of despair blew into him.

It was such an icy blast it brought tears to his eyes, and he had to pull over against the curb. He'd been sure.

He'd been so sure that Jeff was the one behind it all, and he'd been wrong.

Now he had no idea which way to turn, which direction to look for them. He was an FBI agent—a profiler, for God's sake—and he was utterly powerless to help the people he wanted to help most.

Unable to shove down the grief that clawed at him, he lowered his head to the steering wheel.

DANIELLA HAD LOST ALL track of time. She had no idea how long it had been since she'd awakened. Macy had apparently gone back to sleep, for she'd been quiet for the past hour.

She and Macy had talked through the door for a long time, chatting about happy days and favorite things. Daniella had been desperate to waylay any fear that Macy might feel.

Unfortunately nothing she said to Macy diminished the fear that gnawed like cancer inside Daniella. Surely everyone knew by now that they were missing. Sam would be frantic and Jim would be investigating.

But how could they find out who was responsible when *she* didn't even know who it was? How was Sam going to find them when she didn't even know if they were still in Bachelor Moon?

A sound came from outside the door at the end of the room. Somebody was coming! Her heart beat so fast she felt light-headed as she waited to see who was behind the door.

There was the sound of the key in a lock and then the

knob began to turn. Daniella held her breath, wondering what a monster looked like in the flesh.

Frank. The monster looked like Frank. For a moment her brain couldn't make sense of it as he stepped into the room and smiled at her, the same kind of smile he'd given her every day since he'd first come to work for her.

"Ah, you're awake," he said, as if he were greeting her in her own kitchen.

Daniella stood from the bed. "Frank, what's going on? What are we doing here?"

He gestured toward the small table. "Why don't you have a seat?"

She didn't want to sit with him. She wanted to scream. She wanted to throw herself at him and claw out his eyes. But she didn't know his frame of mind, wasn't sure what he was capable of, and the last thing she wanted to do was make him angry with Macy locked behind a door.

Cautiously she moved to the table and sat. He sat across from her and smiled once again. "This has been my dream," he said. "Having you seated across a table from me as we talk about our day."

She couldn't wrap her mind around it. She stared at him blankly. Frank?

"I know I've surprised you with all this, but in time you'll understand that we were meant to be together, the three of us, as a family." He leaned back in the chair, his gaze not leaving her. "I still remember the first time I ever laid eyes on you. You probably don't remember, but Johnny and I were working at the factory and you brought him lunch. You were wearing a light blue blouse and shorts, and I fell in love with you at that very moment."

Daniella didn't know what to say. Words refused to come to her lips, to her brain. She was beyond stunned. Frank had been her right-hand man, the one she depended on to help run the business. He'd been the one who she had counted on to drive Macy to playdates.

He looked at his watch. "I only have a minute or two for now. I just wanted to let you know that the guests have arrived and are all settled in. I've got dinner ready to go. I've got everything under control for you, Daniella."

His words let her know that they were very close to the bed-and-breakfast. "Where exactly is this place, Frank?"

He got up from the table. "Nice, isn't it? It's going to be our new home. It's an underground bunker that I built over the years. We've got everything we need here to make a happy life."

My God, he'd been planning this for years, she thought. "Was it you who attacked me in the bait shack?"

He frowned. "Stupid of me. I thought maybe I could bring you here then, but then Macy showed up and screamed and I had to get out of there fast."

"And you killed Samantha?"

His frown deepened. "That girl was nothing but a piece of trash. She came out to talk to me, told me she'd pay me double what you were paying if I'd come to work for her in her new bed-and-breakfast. She was trouble and she intended to make trouble for you. I couldn't let that happen."

His frown transformed to a smile of delight. "But all's well that ends well. We're together now and eventually you'll love me like I love you."

He was crazy. If he thought he could keep her and Macy down here long enough to make them love him, then he was insane. Not only that, he was dangerous. He'd already killed a woman, and even though she was afraid to ask her next question, she had to know.

"What about Johnny?"

"He wasn't the man for you. He didn't love you like I did. That night he went out to get diapers I met him in the driveway. I told him I was in love with you and he got mad, tried to fire me. I knew I'd never get my dream of being with you unless he was gone. Johnny thought he was big and tough, but I snapped his neck like a twig, then weighed down his body and threw him in the pond. I got in the car and drove it south, left it behind an old abandoned building and then hitched back here."

Grief roared through Daniella. She'd known it; she'd known it all along. Johnny hadn't left her and Macy. He'd been ripped from them by a monster.

"I've got to get back," Frank said, and started for the door.

Daniella jumped up from her chair. "Frank, before you go, will you unlock the door so I can be with Macy? She's afraid, Frank. She needs to be with me."

He nodded and walked toward the door that separated the two rooms. As he bent over the padlock and fumbled with his key ring, Daniella wanted to fling herself on his back, slam him over the head, do whatever it took to destroy him.

He'd snapped Johnny's neck like a twig. Frank had a big chest and strong arms, and she feared that if she attacked him without a weapon he'd win. She didn't want to imagine the consequences.

Instead she watched as he unlocked the door and turned to face her. "As long as you behave yourself like a good woman should, then I'll keep this door unlocked. If you give me trouble, I'll see to it that you and Macy can't be together until you get into line. There's food in the refrigerator. I'll see you tonight."

As he left the room Daniella looked into where Macy was sound asleep on top of the pretty pink bedspread that covered the twin bed. How was she going to tell her that the monster had them and this time no princess crown was going to save them?

Chapter Twelve

For most of the afternoon Sam had driven the streets of Bachelor Moon, looking for something or somebody who could give him a clue as to what had happened to Daniella and Macy.

His heart was nothing more than a cold chunk of ice in his chest. He kept in constant contact with Jim, but the lawman had little comfort to give him. No prints had been lifted from the window where the perpetrator had entered. At least at the moment no evidence had been discovered that might solve the crime.

It was just after dinnertime when Sam pulled back into the driveway of the bed-and-breakfast. Darkness would fall soon, and he couldn't imagine going through a night of not knowing if Daniella and Macy were still alive.

Several strangers sat in the chairs on the porch, and Sam nodded as he went into the house. It appeared like business as usual at the bed-and-breakfast except for the fact that the owner and her daughter had been kidnapped.

Sam found Frank in the kitchen cleaning up after

the evening meal. "Nothing?" Frank asked as he turned around from the sink.

"Nothing," Sam replied flatly.

"I told the guests that she had a family emergency and had to leave town for a few days," Frank said as he plunged his hands into soapy water in the sink. "I figured the littler they knew about what was going on here the better."

Sam watched as Frank moved several large knives and a huge bowl into the water. It should have been Daniella standing in front of the sink.

Maybe everyone had been right about him. Maybe he was so burned out that he was no longer an effective profiler. He couldn't help but believe he'd missed something, that the answers were right in front of him but he couldn't see them.

The worst part was he didn't know what to do to fix this. He didn't know where to look for them, and sitting at the table where he'd spent so many hours with Daniella was a particular form of torture.

Frank finished with the dishes and put them all away except for a small paring knife he carried to the table. "I figured in about an hour I'll head home for the night. I told the guests if they needed anything you'd be around. I hope that's okay."

Sam nodded. "I guess I'll be around. I don't know where else to go."

Frank sank down in the chair opposite Sam. "Jim and his men checked out the property, including my place.

When he left here he said he intended to do a house-by-house search in town."

"You thinking about stabbing me?" Sam asked as he gestured toward the knife.

"Nah, this thing is dull. I'm going to take it back to my place and sharpen it. I have a whetstone I use to give everything around here a really sharp edge." Frank leaned forward. "Jim will find them. Somebody has to find them."

Once again a wind of despair whispered through Sam. He'd worked enough cases in his career to know that wasn't necessarily true. Sometimes people disappeared forever.

"Have you eaten?" Frank asked. "There's some leftover roast in the fridge. I could make you a sandwich."

"No thanks, Frank. I'm not hungry." Although he hadn't eaten all day, his stomach was far too twisted in knots to want any food.

"I'm going to go check on all the guests and then I guess I'll call it a night. I'll be back here around six in the morning to get started on breakfast." He rose from the table, grabbed the knife and put it in his pocket.

As he left the room Sam leaned back in his chair and released a deep sigh. He knew from talking to Jim that afternoon that nothing had been found at Matt's house in town, that Frank's cottage hadn't yielded anything, and he himself knew that Jeff wasn't responsible. So who?

It had been his experience that often stalkers who

left gifts hung around to see the response of the person receiving those gifts. They were embroiled in the life of the person they professed to love.

Jim had told Sam he'd assigned several deputies to check out the people who made regular deliveries to the bed-and-breakfast. Sam couldn't fault Jim's investigation.

He faulted himself for not seeing this coming, for not thinking that it was possible for somebody to crawl silently through a window and whisk away the two people he loved.

Love. The alien emotion welled up inside him, bringing new tears to his eyes. He loved Daniella and Macy like he'd never loved before in his life, and the fact that they were in trouble or could already be dead nearly broke him.

He would have never done anything to follow up on his love for them, but he wanted them safe, here where they belonged. When he went back to Kansas City he needed to know that they were building their happy life here. He had to believe they were still alive.

He rubbed a hand across his forehead, where a headache was starting to pound. He closed his eyes and allowed everything that had happened over the past two weeks to fly through his head.

It had all begun with Samantha's murder. As Jim had said, she'd been killed with an ordinary butcher knife as sharp as a scalpel.

I have a whetstone I use to give everything around here a really sharp edge. Frank's words rolled around in Sam's brain and he snapped his eyes open, headache forgotten.

That's what I do, I take care of things for Daniella.

Was it possible that the culprit had been under their noses all the time? But Jim had checked Frank's cottage and Daniella and Macy hadn't been there, a little voice protested.

But maybe he has them stashed someplace else. Thoughts whirled through Sam's head at a dizzying speed. That day that Daniella had been attacked in the bait shack Frank had come running from the direction of the pond.

Was it possible he'd attacked her, then run in that direction only to run back when Macy had screamed? Had he hurried back to make sure that Macy wouldn't be able to identify him?

For the first time since he'd left Jeff's house a burst of adrenaline surged up inside him. He got up from the table and moved to the door of the common room, where Frank was telling several of the guests goodbye for the night.

Living so close to the main house it would have been easy for Frank to leave the gifts on the porch without being seen. He took care of things for Daniella—things like weeding and cutting brush and killing Samantha.

Sam's blood ran cold. It was possible that he was wrong about Frank. But it was also possible that he was right. There was only one way to find out. He had to follow Frank and see if during the night he might lead Sam to wherever he had Daniella and Macy stashed.

The worst that could happen was that Sam would lose some time, but at the moment time was all he had, time and the burning need to find Daniella and Macy.

When Frank finally went out the front door to head home, Sam waited a couple of minutes and then stepped out on the porch. He could see the man making his way toward the cottage in the distance, and after another minute Sam followed.

He moved silently through the grass, trying to use the trees and overgrown brush as cover in case Frank happened to look behind him.

When Frank disappeared into the small cottage he called his, Sam took up residency behind a nearby large tree trunk. He sank to the ground and stared at the cottage.

Maybe this was nothing more than a wild-goose chase. But somehow, as he'd put all the pieces together, all the fingers on the hand of accusation pointed to Frank as a major suspect.

Frank would have known that the windows in Macy's room were accessible. Even if Macy had awakened she wouldn't have screamed at the sight of her buddy Frank in her room.

It all made a horrifying kind of sense.

Sam leaned with his head back against the trunk. The only thing he could hope at this point was that Frank would eventually lead him to them.

He had to believe they were close. Sam looked around the area. Thick woods surrounded Frank's cottage and extended to someplace unknown to Sam. It was possible there was a shed, a shanty or some other structure where they could be kept on the property or nearby on somebody else's property.

Darkness was starting to fall, and Sam felt it in his bones, in his heart. Was Macy someplace in the dark? Afraid of monsters and without her princess crown?

Sam was a monster chaser, a monster destroyer, and he prayed that he was on the right track here with Frank. He knew more than anyone that monsters could wear a variety of disguises. They could be ex-boyfriends, coworkers or fathers. They could be the neighbor, the preacher's son or a handyman.

When darkness came it slammed down and shrouded everything except a small light coming from the front window of the cottage.

Sam had known grief before. After the traumatic death of his mother he'd grieved long and hard. But he didn't remember it being as intense, as devastating, as what he felt now.

He shifted positions, wondering if he'd made yet another mistake, if maybe he was wasting precious time that could be spent elsewhere.

He wasn't sure how long he sat behind the tree trunk, his heart filled with thoughts of Daniella and Macy, when the door to Frank's cottage opened.

In the spill of light that seeped out on the porch Sam saw Frank leaving the place. Instantly adrenaline pumped through Sam. He crouched, ready to shadow the man, who clicked on a flashlight as he left the porch.

Where would Frank be going at this time of night with

a flashlight in hand? He certainly wasn't headed back toward the house, but rather deeper into the woods.

Frank's flashlight made it easy for Sam to follow him, although he moved cautiously so as not to make any noise that might alert Frank to his presence.

Sam's heart beat so hard, so fast, he wondered how Frank couldn't hear it. And as he followed, he felt the beginning stirrings of rage inside him.

Frank stopped and Sam froze, holding his breath as he waited to see what Frank's next move would be. To Sam's shock he reached down and lifted what looked like a door in the ground, then he disappeared from Sam's sight.

Sam waited a heart-stopping moment before he hurried to where he'd last seen Frank. Wooden stairs led down to a door that was now closed.

A homemade cellar, that's what it was, similar to what were found on many old farms in the Midwest. Sam's first instinct was to race down the stairs and storm inside, but he had no idea what he'd be rushing into, and the last thing he wanted was to put Daniella and Macy in further danger.

Instead he pulled out his cell phone and dialed Jim Thompson's number. "Jim," he said softly into the phone when the sheriff answered, "Frank has them. I don't know if they're alive or not, but he's got them in an underground cellar of some kind just north of his cottage. He's down there now, and I'm waiting for him to come back up. If you aren't here quick enough, by the time you arrive you're going to have to arrest me for murder—for real this time."

Sam clicked off the phone, pulled his gun and sat to wait.

Each minute that passed was torture. He had no idea what was happening belowground, no idea if Frank had killed them and buried them in this place. The one thing he knew with certainty was if Frank had hurt or killed either one of the females Sam loved, Frank would never live to see the morning light.

The beam of a flashlight in the distance let him know that Jim had arrived. Sam rose to his feet and hurried to meet him.

"Do I need to use my cuffs on you?" Jim asked in a pseudowhisper.

"Not yet. He's still down there. I don't know if Daniella and Macy are okay or not." Sam kept his voice equally low.

"You sure they're in there?" Jim looked old and tired in the glow from his flashlight.

"What else would he be doing out here after dark? If he dug out this cellar, then he's been planning this for a very long time." Sam's stomach ached with anxiety.

"Should we go in? Between the two of us we can take him down," Jim said. "And Deputy Wilkerson should be here soon, as well."

More than anything Sam wanted to rush down those stairs, burst through the door and see if Daniella and Macy were alive and well. But he was terrified of the consequences of such actions without knowing specifically what was on the other side of the closed door at the bottom of the stairs.

"I think we need to wait until he comes back up. If Daniella and Macy are down there I don't want to turn this into some kind of a hostage situation. I believe he killed Samantha, and that means he's capable of anything."

"Then we wait," Jim agreed, and clicked off the beam of his light.

Sam had never known that minutes could creep by so slowly, that an hour could feel like an eternity, but as he and Jim waited for Frank to resurface, time seemed to stand still.

Deputy Wilkerson arrived and took up a position on the other side of the door, and they waited some more. Sam's head filled with horrifying images.

What was happening below the ground? Had he raped Daniella? Had he killed them both and was he now merely visiting their bodies?

The serial killer Jeffrey Dahmer had killed his victims and saved parts of them so they would be with him forever. Did Frank have the same kind of brain disconnect?

As they waited he told Jim in hushed whispers what had made him suspect Frank in the first place, and after that the men fell silent.

Sam was just about to explode with his need to do something when he heard the sound of the door at the bottom of the stairs creaking open and then closed.

Footsteps scraped against the wooden stairs, and then

he appeared. Sam didn't wait. With a roar of rage he threw himself at Frank.

Frank yelped in surprise and kicked at Sam's gun hand. The gun flew from Sam's grasp and into the darkness, but that didn't slow Sam.

His first punch clipped Frank's chin and his second landed square in the man's stomach. Sam was aware of Jim calling out for him to stop, but he didn't want to stop. He wanted to hurt Frank, to punish him.

"They're mine!" Frank screamed. He managed to hit Sam with a fist on the side of the face. Sam reeled backward and then lunged once again, this time tumbling himself and Frank to the ground. Sam felt more than a little bit crazy as he pummeled Frank. The monster he'd always feared resided inside him was loose.

"Stop it. Damn it, stop it, both of you!" Jim yelled. "Don't make me shoot you both."

Deputy Wilkerson pulled at the back of Sam's shirt in an effort to get him off Frank. Sanity returned to Sam and he got up.

Wilkerson pulled Frank up off the ground. His nose was bloody and one of his eyes was already beginning to blacken, but he smiled at Sam. "You'll never have them. They're my family. They'll always belong to me."

His words iced Sam's heart as Wilkerson slapped cuffs on Frank. "He should have keys on him," Sam said. Wilkerson dug in Frank's pocket and pulled out a set of keys, then tossed them to Sam.

His fingers trembled as he raced to the top of the

stairs. *Let them be okay,* he prayed as he stumbled down to the door. *Please let them be safe and sound.*

They'll always belong to me.

Frank's words roared in Sam's head as he fumbled to find the right key to unlock the door. When he finally unlocked it, he eased the door open.

Shock ricocheted through him as he saw the space on the other side of the door. It was an entire room, like an efficiency apartment.

And it was empty.

He nearly fell to his knees. If they weren't here, then where? He saw another door and, numb with grief, he moved on wooden feet toward it.

He froze in the doorway. Daniella and Macy were curled together on a small bed, and for one agonizing moment he thought they were dead. "No." The protest fell from his lips. Although it was nothing more than a mere whisper it thundered in the silence of the room.

Daniella and Macy jumped up. "Mr. Sam!" Macy cried, and scrambled off the bed to race toward him.

Sam heaved a deep breath and captured her to his chest. He picked her up in one arm and by that time Daniella was in his other. He squeezed them tight against him as tears momentarily blurred his vision. At that moment Jim appeared in the doorway.

"I knew you'd come," Macy exclaimed as Sam set her back on the floor. He didn't release Daniella. He couldn't. He needed to breathe in the scent of her, feel the warmth of her body to assure him that she was really okay.

She made no move to leave the safety of his arm

around her. She leaned into him, and he felt the tremors that shook her body.

"Thank God," Jim said. "Thank God you're both safe."

"It was Frank," Daniella said. "He took us while we slept and brought us here. He wanted us to be his family. He was crazy." The words tumbled out of her as if forced by pressure. "He murdered Samantha and he killed Johnny."

"He was a monster," Macy said, her eyes wide. "He was a bad monster."

"We caught the monster, Macy. He won't ever bother you again," Sam replied. "Let's get you two out of here."

As they climbed up the stairs out of the dungeon of Frank's madness, Sam realized that he'd found them just in time to tell them goodbye.

Chapter Thirteen

The night went on forever for Daniella. She was taken by Jim to the sheriff's office, where both she and Macy were interviewed about everything that had taken place with Frank.

Sam hadn't come, and she ached with the need to be held in his arms as she relived the horror of that time in the underground cellar.

It was almost two in the morning by the time Jim took them back to the bed-and-breakfast. Macy fell asleep on the drive back, and when they reached the driveway Daniella's heart expanded as Sam stepped out on the porch.

He looked big and strong in the silhouette from the porch light as he walked out to meet them. When he saw the sleeping child in the backseat, he opened the door and gently lifted Macy into his arms.

"I'll be in touch if I need anything else," Jim said as Daniella got out of the passenger seat. "Daniella, I'm sorry about everything. You know, I'm sorry about Johnny."

She nodded and then closed the door and followed

Sam into the house. He carried Macy into her bedroom and gently placed her on the bed. Macy didn't stir.

As he walked out of her bedroom Daniella went directly into his arms and began to softly cry. She'd held the tears in during her captivity, not wanting Macy to see her cry, but now she could no longer hold back her tears.

"Shh," Sam said as he smoothed his hands down her back. "It's over now. You're safe. Frank can never bother you again."

She nodded. She knew all that, but the knowledge didn't stop the tears of fear and relief, and finally of grief. Her emotions were a jumble, and it was impossible to pick any one that was stronger than the other.

All she knew was that she never wanted to move from Sam's embrace, that she needed him to hold her until the morning finally came.

He finally stepped back from her as her tears began to ebb. "Come on, let's get you into bed. It's been a long night."

Wearily she went into her bedroom and pulled her nightgown from her drawer. "I want…I need to shower," she said, desperate to somehow wash off the night's events and be fresh.

Sam took her by the shoulders, his eyes as dark as the night outside the windows. "Daniella, did he touch you?" His voice was thick with emotion.

"No." She shook her head quickly. "No, he didn't touch me or Macy. I just need to feel clean again." He dropped his hands to his sides, and she went into the bathroom.

Once in the shower she allowed the hot water to spray over her as her mind played and replayed everything that had happened. She was viscerally aware that if Sam hadn't figured out that Frank was the guilty party, she and Macy might have never been found.

It's over, she told herself. *There's nothing to be afraid of anymore.* She had a houseful of guests for the weekend, and life would go back to normal.

She turned off the water, dried and then pulled on her nightgown. Life *was* returning to normal, but at the moment she still felt vulnerable, shaken by what had happened.

Sam was sitting on the edge of the bed as she returned to the room. He rose as she entered, and at that moment she realized she was going to lose him, that now that the danger had passed he would leave.

"Hold me through the night?" she asked.

He nodded.

She got into bed, and a moment later he joined her. She snuggled into his arms and felt as if she was home. They didn't speak, nor did she try to start any deeper intimacy.

It was enough to be close enough to him that his heart beat against hers, that the achingly familiar scent of him seemed to wrap her in a bubble of warmth and security.

The danger was over and soon the heartache would begin. For now she just wanted to exist in the limbo of the moment. She fell asleep almost immediately and awoke at dawn alone in the bed.

Reaching her hand over to the pillow that Sam had used the night before, she felt the warmth of him still retained there. He must have awakened just before she did.

Her heart already felt his absence, an empty ache she knew would be with her for a very long time. Time to get up and get to business as usual, she told herself. At least for the weekend, hopefully, she wouldn't have too much time to focus on the fact that Sam might leave at any moment.

The morning flew by with breakfast and Daniella getting acquainted with the guests she hadn't met the day before. She hadn't intended to tell anyone about what had happened, but once Macy was up the little girl told everyone that they'd been kidnapped by a monster and Mr. Sam had saved them.

Sam didn't make an appearance until just after lunch. Daniella was in the kitchen when he appeared in the doorway, his suitcase in hand. Even though she knew this was coming, Daniella's heart crashed to the floor.

"So it's time," she said softly.

He nodded, his eyes dark and unreadable. "I'd like to tell Macy goodbye, too."

"I'll go get her and we'll meet you at your car."

A few minutes later Daniella and Macy walked outside where Sam stood beside his car. His suitcase had already been stowed and his hands were in his pockets.

He looked so handsome, with his dark hair gleaming

in the sunshine and his handsome feature schooled in somber lines. He was just supposed to be a guest leaving after his visit, but he'd become so much more to Daniella.

"Mr. Sam, don't go." Macy ran to him and threw her arms around his waist. "Stay here and be my new daddy. My old daddy isn't lost anymore, but he's dead. I want you to stay."

Sam looked tortured as he bent down to one knee and pulled Macy into a hug against his chest. "Honey, I can't stay here. I have to go home."

"Why can't you make this your home?" Tears trekked down Macy's cheeks. "It's a good home, and we'd take good care of you."

Sam stood as if he couldn't stand it anymore. "I have to go. I'm sorry, Macy."

With loud, choking sobs Macy turned and ran back toward the house and disappeared inside. "I'm sorry," Sam said to Daniella.

"She'll be fine. Kids are resilient." Her voice cracked as she felt her own tears rising precariously close to the surface. "Oh, Sam, I don't want you to go, either."

"I have to," he said with a fervent tone. "I can't be a part of this. I can't be a part of you and Macy."

"Why not?" She knew with a woman's heart that he loved her. Why couldn't he accept love in his life? Why was he so determined to be alone?

He stared out into the distance, as if he hadn't heard her question. When he finally looked back at her there was a burn in his eyes that spoke of deep, inner torment.

"Don't you get it? When I got hold of Frank it was like something wild unleashed inside me. I smashed his face and would have beaten him to death if Jim hadn't been there to stop me."

"And I would have clawed his eyes out and smashed his face if I'd had the physical strength to do it," she countered. "What does that have to do with love? What does that have to do with us?"

"Because I'm afraid." The words blurted out of him with a stunning force. He drew in a deep breath as if to steady himself. "Because I'm afraid that I'm my father's son, that there is a monster inside *me* that might someday harm the people closest to me." His eyes now held the hollowness of a broken man.

"Oh, Sam, you couldn't be more wrong." She stepped closer to him and reached up to place her palm against his cheek. "I've seen your heart. I know what's inside you. You are your *mother's* son."

Macy came running back out the door and toward them, her princess crown in hand. Tears still raced down her cheeks as she stopped before Sam. "You told me you chase monsters. You need to take this, Mr. Sam." She held the crown out to him.

"Honey, I can't take that," Sam said, his voice thick and deep with emotion.

"You have to," Macy said, shoving it toward him once again. "It will keep you safe against the monsters. Take it with you so I'm not scared for you."

In obvious reluctance Sam took the crown. "A monster wouldn't win the heart of a little girl, he wouldn't win her princess crown," Daniella said.

He didn't say another word, but turned on his heel, got into his car and just that quickly he was gone.

Macy ran back into the house but Daniella stood and stared after him until his car was no longer visible. She'd known it was going to hurt, to tell him goodbye. But she hadn't anticipated the depth of her pain.

It lanced her like a sword through her center, and the worst part of all was the reason he'd told her goodbye. Because he feared he might be a monster, because he feared he was his father's son.

Her gaze moved to the pond that she now knew was her husband's final resting place. Jim had indicated that they would drag the pond in the next week to bring up the body of the man Daniella had once loved. Johnny's parents had died in a car accident a year after he and Daniella had married. Thankfully they would never know the horror that befell their son.

The grief she felt when she thought about Johnny was distant, not a fresh emotion. She'd grieved deeply for him a long time ago. There was some satisfaction in knowing that he hadn't willingly left her, that he'd died loving her.

One man who loved her had been wrenched from her through murder, and the other who loved her had chosen to walk away from her in some misguided belief that he might hurt her.

With a sigh, she turned and went back into the house.

She had dinner to prepare and guests that needed attention. There wasn't time for a broken heart now. Later, she knew, the full devastation of Sam's absence would haunt her.

SAM HAD HUNG THE PRINCESS crown on his rearview mirror, but after driving almost a hundred miles he took it down and tossed it onto the seat next to him. He couldn't stand looking at it and remembering Macy's tears.

He couldn't stand to see it and think about Daniella. Had he made a mistake? Had he just made the biggest mistake in his life by leaving them?

He could be happy in Bachelor Moon. He could be happy with Daniella and Macy. He'd never thought about happiness before, but he recognized that there had been times over the last two weeks that he'd felt it in his heart, in his very soul.

"You are your mother's son."

Daniella's words reverberated around and around in his head. It was an alien way of thinking to him. It had always been his father who had taken front and center in his mind.

He consciously willed away thoughts of Daniella and Macy and turned on the radio. He had a long drive ahead of him, and he'd made his decision. He refused to second-guess himself.

He drove straight through to Kansas City and arrived at his apartment just after two in the morning. As he walked in the door the silence, the utter lack of life energy, greeted him instead of a welcome sense of homecoming.

Falling into bed, he slept deeply and dreamlessly until seven the next morning. After a long hot shower and a breakfast of coffee and a frozen bagel zapped in the microwave, he headed into FBI headquarters.

The first thing he'd seen as he'd gotten dressed was the princess crown that Macy had given him sitting on top of his dresser. The sight of it had shot a pain so sharp through his center that he'd momentarily thought he might be having a heart attack. Over, he'd told himself as he'd left the room. It was over and it was time for him to move on.

Officially he wasn't back on the job yet. He'd have to get an okay from his supervisor before officially being back, but he wanted to touch base with Lexie Forbes and thank her for taking care of the background searches he'd needed.

He found Lexie in the area the other agents called the dungeon, a portion of the building's basement that housed the computer geeks.

Lexie Forbes was easy to find, with the neon pink streak in her light brown hair and the oversized black-rimmed glasses that didn't quite hide the spring green of her eyes.

She was a favorite among the agents. Scary bright, quirky as hell, she was constantly looking for the man of her dreams in a string of losers who couldn't look past the charming quirks that made her intriguing.

She saw him and offered him a welcoming smile.

"Look who's back. The Prince of Darkness has returned to the building." She pulled off the headset she'd been wearing and whirled her computer chair around to face him. "How was your vacation?"

Emotional, filled with danger, in some ways devastating—that was what flew through his head, but he didn't say it. "Okay. How are things here? You find Mr. Right yet?"

"A mythical creature," she replied. "I figure I'll give it two more years, but if I haven't found him by my thirtieth birthday I'm getting artificially inseminated and creating my own family."

Sam smiled, although the gesture couldn't begin to lighten his heart, which still held the deep bruising of heartbreak. "I just wanted to stop by and thank you for helping me out while I was gone."

Lexie shrugged her shoulders. "Not a problem, just a matter of a few keystrokes here and there." Sam knew it was more complicated than that, but he didn't protest. "You back on the job?"

"Don't know yet. I have to talk to the man and see if he thinks I'm ready to come back. I hope so. I can't stand my own company." What he couldn't stand was having any downtime that might give him an opportunity to think about the two females he'd left behind.

"I dunno, Sam. You don't look that rested or revitalized to me," Lexie observed, as she squinted at him.

He certainly felt older, more tired, than he had when he'd left here. "All I need is to get back to work," he said firmly. With a nod of goodbye he went in search of his boss.

Work was what he needed to get the mental vision of Daniella out of his head. He had to forget how she'd looked that last moment he'd seen her, with a sheen of tears shining in her beautiful blue eyes, with the glow of the sun on her hair.

He needed to forget how she'd felt naked in his arms, sweetly gasping his name as they'd made love. He desperately needed to forget that look she sometimes had in her eyes when she gazed at him, a look that had spoken of respect and invitation and so much love.

He had to forget that he'd ever gone to a place called Bachelor Moon. The Prince of Darkness rode through life alone; that was all he needed to remember.

DANIELLA STOOD AT THE back door and stared out unseeing as she sipped a cup of coffee. The sun had lowered in the sky, painting an early evening golden glow to the landscape.

It had been a week since Sam had left, and each day she hoped the pain inside her would ease, but so far that hadn't happened.

Even Macy had remained unusually subdued over the past week. When Sam had driven away he'd left a huge void behind, and it was just going to take time for that void to be filled.

There were no guests in the house at the moment. Yesterday there had been a memorial service for Johnny by the pond. Daniella had been pleased that it seemed the whole town had turned out to show their support and pay their respects.

As she'd listened to Reverend David St. James talk about what a good man Johnny had been, how he'd been a devoted husband and father, the final piece of closure had washed over Daniella.

Johnny had gone to his watery grave loving her, and now she had all the answers she needed concerning his disappearance and was at peace.

With a deep sigh she turned away from the door and instead set her coffee cup down and went in search of Macy. She found her in her bedroom playing with her fashion dolls.

"Look, this is Mr. Sam," Macy said as she held up a handsome, dark-haired doll.

Daniella forced a smile to her lips. "He looks very nice in his tuxedo."

Macy set the doll on the floor. "I miss him."

"I know, honey—so do I."

Macy frowned. "He wasn't very good at fishing, but he was good at everything else. I could have taught him how to fish better if he'd stayed a while longer."

"It will soon be time for you to put your dolls away and get into the bathtub."

The ring of the business phone pulled Daniella from the room. She hurried into the kitchen and answered. "Bachelor Moon Bed and Breakfast."

"Daniella."

His voice washed over her in a shower of warmth and she squeezed the receiver closer to her ear. "Sam."

Her heart instantly stepped up its rhythm even as she told herself she was a fool. He was probably calling because he thought he'd left something here or he had some paperwork to fill out and needed some answers from her.

"How are things going?" he asked.

"Fine. Just fine." She tried to put a lilt in her tone. She didn't want him to know how difficult it was for her just to hear the sound of his voice.

"I have some things to follow up on and was wondering if you could meet me at Mama's Café."

Her heart rate stepped up once again. Sam was here in town? She didn't want to see him again. It would hurt too much, and yet her heart ached with the need to look at him again. "When?"

"Now…or as soon as possible," he replied.

Her mind whirled. "It might take me a while to get there. I need to see if I can get somebody to watch Macy." There was no way she wanted her daughter to know that Sam was back in town. There was no way she wanted Macy to have any interaction with him. As difficult as it was going to be for Daniella, it would be devastating for Macy to have to tell him goodbye yet again.

"However long it takes, I'll be waiting." He clicked off, and Daniella immediately called Tina and arranged for Macy to stay with her for a couple of hours. Within thirty minutes Daniella was alone in the car and headed from Tina's to Mama's Café.

She told herself there was no reason to entertain any

kind of hope in her heart. There had been nothing in his voice to indicate that this was anything but some sort of business that needed to be taken care of.

Still, that hadn't stopped her from putting on her prettiest pink lipstick and an extra coat of mascara before she'd left the house.

As she turned down Main Street she tried to calm the jittering of her nerves. He probably had some sort of paperwork to fill out because of what had happened while he was here on vacation.

Still, as she pulled into a parking space in front of the café and saw him standing out front, she couldn't stop the soaring of her heart.

Clad in a pair of jeans and a navy T-shirt, he looked achingly handsome. In his hand he held Macy's crown, and she wondered if that was what had brought him back here—the need to return a little girl's crown.

She got out of her car and forced a smile to her lips. "Hey, Mr. Sam."

"Daniella." He met her at the car door and held out the crown toward her. "Put this in your car and take it back to Macy. I just borrowed it—it was never mine to keep."

Her initial reaction was to protest, but there was a tremble in his voice that kept her silent. She took the crown from him and tossed it onto her passenger seat, then turned back to face him.

Had he driven all these miles for no other reason? Her heart now had the same empty echo that she'd felt the day he'd driven away from the bed-and-breakfast.

"Take a walk with me?" he asked.

She nodded, her emotion too thick in her throat to speak. They fell into step side by side and headed toward the park in the center square.

"I heard you had a memorial service for Johnny," he said, and gestured to a bench.

"Yes, it was nice. Everyone has been very supportive." They sat, not quite touching but close enough that she could smell his familiar scent.

There was a long moment of silence and she jumped to fill it. "Jeff and Tina have started dating, and I'm so pleased for both of them. Hopefully they can make it work. They both deserve to find happiness with somebody. Matt moved out and seems happy in his new place. What are you doing here, Sam?"

The question fell from her lips before she realized she was going to ask it. But it was a catalyst that forced her emotions to the surface. She gazed at him, his features easily discernible in both the moonlight and the glow of a nearby streetlamp.

"Why are you here? You could have just mailed that crown back to Macy if that's what you wanted to do. Why are you here with me now?" She recognized a hint of anger in her voice.

He knew how she felt about him. How dare he come back here and break her heart all over again just by his mere sight? Didn't he realize that sitting here next to him, smelling his cologne, feeling the warmth of his body radiating toward her, was torture?

He gazed out into the distance. "I was so sure that

I made the right choice when I left here. I drove away certain that I could put my time here, my time with you and Macy, behind me."

He turned to look at her and his eyes glowed with an emotion she couldn't identify. "I've always been able to lose myself in my work, but this time was different. All I kept thinking about was you and Macy and my father and the kind of man I believed myself to be."

"I know the man you are," Daniella said, hope beginning to glow like a candle inside her heart. "You're the kind of man I love…strong and funny, caring and passionate."

The candle flickered hesitantly as he once again directed his gaze to the distance. "I finally decided to do what I do best—profile a killer."

Her gaze turned to confusion. "What do you mean?"

Once again he looked at her, and his eyes held a hint of the darkness that surrounded them. "I've always been afraid that like my father, there was a killer hiding deep inside me just waiting for the right moment to spring out of the shadows, and so I profiled myself."

"And what did you find?" She reached for his hand, unable to deny herself physical contact with him for another moment.

"I discovered that I'm an ordinary man who has tried for years to understand what drove my father to do what he did on that terrible day so long ago. I realized that you were right—I'm not my father's son. I don't have the capacity to harm somebody I love."

His fingers tightened around hers as he continued.

"I learned I have a great capacity to love a little girl who has the best princess walk in the world and thinks fireflies are the prettiest bugs God ever made. More than that, I realized I'm tired of living in the darkness, that I need more in my life, that I need you."

He stood from the bench and pulled her to her feet. She flew into his arms, her heart beating wildly and the candle glow a raging fire of love. "I love you, Daniella, and I can't imagine living another second of my life without you."

His mouth took hers in a kiss that fed the hunger in her soul, that soothed the ache in her heart and that tasted not only of his passion, but of her own, as well.

When the kiss ended he took her hand, and they walked a couple of steps. Then he halted and faced the statue of the town founder, Larry Bridges. He drew Daniella back into his arms and smiled down at her.

"Look up," he said.

She tilted her head back and gasped as she saw the full moon overhead. "It's a Bachelor Moon," she said, her heart beating wildly in her chest.

"And I'm standing in the place where the legend begins, a confirmed bachelor who knows now what it's like to love, to be loved. I don't want to be a bachelor anymore, Daniella."

Her heart swelled with happiness, but there was an issue that forced her to hold off embracing her own joy. "Sam, what about your job?"

"I'm done with it. I've already tendered my resignation. I heard there might be an opening at the Bachelor

Moon Bed and Breakfast for a handyman. The pay isn't great but the fringe benefits are amazing."

She laughed, but then sobered quickly. There was no way a man like Sam Connelly would be content working as a handyman. "That would be nice for a while, but then what?"

"I was thinking maybe I'd make a run for the position of sheriff. With Jim retiring, the town is going to need a new sheriff."

"And you're just the man to fit the job," she said, the last of her reservations melting away. She reached up and wrapped her arms around his neck and smiled as he pulled her closer against him. "I love you, Sam." The words seemed inadequate for the feelings she held in her heart.

"And I love you, Daniella. You have healed my darkness and filled my heart with light." Once again their mouths met in a fiery kiss that left her breathless.

"Where's Macy?" he asked when the kiss ended.

"At Tina's."

"We'd better go get her and tell her she's getting her wish," he said, as they began to walk toward their cars. "She's going to get me as a daddy."

Daniella knew Macy would be as over the moon as she was. As she got into her car she looked up again. Yes, they were all over the moon, the Bachelor Moon that had brought them all love forevermore.

* * * * *

INTRIGUE

COMING NEXT MONTH

Available March 8, 2011

#1263 RANSOM FOR A PRINCE
Cowboys Royale
Lisa Childs

#1264 AK-COWBOY
Sons of Troy Ledger
Joanna Wayne

#1265 THE SECRET OF CYPRIERE BAYOU
Shivers
Jana DeLeon

#1266 PROTECTING PLAIN JANE
The Precinct: SWAT
Julie Miller

#1267 NAVY SEAL SECURITY
Brothers in Arms
Carol Ericson

#1268 CIRCUMSTANTIAL MARRIAGE
Thriller
Kerry Connor

HICNM0211

USA TODAY *bestselling author Lynne Graham*
is back with a thrilling new trilogy
SECRETLY PREGNANT, CONVENIENTLY WED

Three heroines must marry alpha males to keep
their dreams...but Alejandro, Angelo and Cesario
are not about to be tamed!

Book 1—JEMIMA'S SECRET
Available March 2011 from Harlequin Presents®.

JEMIMA yanked open a drawer in the sideboard to find
Alfie's birth certificate. Her son was her husband's child.
It was a question of telling the truth whether she liked it or
not. She extended the certificate to Alejandro.

"This has to be nonsense," Alejandro asserted.

"Well, if you can find some other way of explaining how
I managed to give birth by that date and Alfie not be yours,
I'd like to hear it," Jemima challenged.

Alejandro glanced up, golden eyes bright as blades and
as dangerous. "All this proves is that you must still have
been pregnant when you walked out on our marriage. It
does not automatically follow that the child is mine."

"'I know it doesn't suit you to hear this news now and I
really didn't want to tell you. But I can't lie to you about it.
Someday Alfie may want to look you up and get acquainted."

"If what you have just told me is the truth, if that little
boy does prove to be mine, it was vindictive and extremely
selfish of you to leave me in ignorance!"

Jemima paled. "When I left you, I had no idea that I was
still pregnant."

"Two years is a long period of time, yet you made no
attempt to inform me that I might be a father. I will want
DNA tests to confirm your claim before I make any deci-

sion about what I want to do."

"Do as you like," she told him curtly. "*I* know who Alfie's father is and there has never been any doubt of his identity."

"I will make arrangements for the tests to be carried out and I will see you again when the result is available," Alejandro drawled with lashings of dark Spanish masculine reserve.

"I'll contact a solicitor and start the divorce," Jemima proffered in turn.

Alejandro's eyes narrowed in a piercing scrutiny that made her uncomfortable. "It would be foolish to do anything before we have that DNA result."

"I disagree," Jemima flashed back. "I should have applied for a divorce the minute I left you!"

Alejandro quirked an ebony brow. "And why didn't you?"

Jemima dealt him a fulminating glance but said nothing, merely moving past him to open her front door in a blunt invitation for him to leave.

"I'll be in touch," he delivered on the doorstep.

What is Alejandro's next move? Perhaps rekindling their marriage is the only solution! But will Jemima agree?

Find out in Lynne Graham's
exciting new romance
JEMIMA'S SECRET

Available March 2011
from Harlequin Presents®.

Start your Best Body today with these top 3 nutrition tips!

1. SHOP THE PERIMETER OF THE GROCERY STORE: The good stuff—fruits, veggies, lean proteins and dairy—always line the outer edges of the store. When you veer into the center aisles, you enter the temptation zone, where the unhealthy foods live.

2. WATCH PORTION SIZES: Most portion sizes in restaurants are nearly twice the size of a true serving and at home, it's easy to "clean your plate." Use these easy serving guidelines:
- Protein: the palm of your hand
- Grains or Fruit: a cup of your hand
- Veggies: the palm of two open hands

3. USE THE RAINBOW RULE FOR PRODUCE: Your produce drawers should be filled with every color of fruits and vegetables. The greater the variety, the more vitamins and other nutrients you add to your diet.

Find these and many more helpful tips in

YOUR BEST BODY NOW
by
TOSCA RENO
WITH STACY BAKER

Bestselling Author of
THE EAT-CLEAN DIET®

Available wherever books are sold!

NTRSERIESFEB

PRESENTING...THE SEVENTH ANNUAL
MORE THAN WORDS™ ANTHOLOGY

Five bestselling authors
Five real-life heroines

This year's Harlequin More Than Words award recipients have changed lives, one good deed at a time. To celebrate these real-life heroines, some of Harlequin's most acclaimed authors have honored the winners by writing stories inspired by these dedicated women. Within the pages of *More Than Words Volume 7*, you will find novellas written by Carly Phillips, Donna Hill and Jill Shalvis—and online at www.HarlequinMoreThanWords.com you can also access stories by Pamela Morsi and Meryl Sawyer.

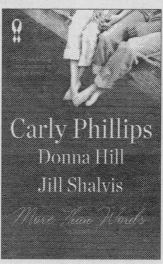

Coming soon in print and online!

Visit
www.HarlequinMoreThanWords.com
to access your FREE ebooks and to nominate a real-life heroine in your community.

Proceeds from the sale of this book will be reinvested in Harlequin's charitable initiatives.

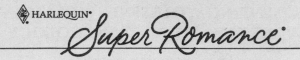

Top author
Janice Kay Johnson
brings readers a riveting new romance
with
Bone Deep

Kathryn Riley is the prime suspect in
the case of her husband's disappearance
four years ago—that is, until someone tries
to make her disappear...forever. Now
handsome police chief Grant Haller must
stop suspecting Kathryn and instead begin
to protect her. But can Grant put aside the
growing feelings for Kathryn long enough
to catch the real criminal?

Find out in March.

*Available wherever
books are sold.*